Eternal Guardians ; bk. 8.85
1001 Dark Nights

P9-CND-244

Ensnared

Also from Elisabeth Naughton

Eternal Guardians
(paranormal romance)
MARKED
ENTWINED
TEMPTED
ENRAPTURED
ENSLAVED
BOUND
TWISTED
RAVAGED
AWAKENED
UNCHAINED
HUNTED
ENSNARED

Firebrand Series
(paranormal romance)
BOUND TO SEDUCTION
SLAVE TO PASSION
POSSESSED BY DESIRE

Against All Odds Series
(romantic suspense)
WAIT FOR ME
HOLD ON TO ME
MELT FOR ME

Aegis Series
(romantic suspense)
FIRST EXPOSURE
SINFUL SURRENDER
EXTREME MEASURES
LETHAL CONSEQUENCES
FATAL PURSUIT

Ensnared

An Eternal Guardians Novella

By Elisabeth Naughton

1001 Dark Nights

EVIL EYE
CONCEPTS

Henderson County Public Library

Ensnared
An Eternal Guardians Novella
By Elisabeth Naughton

1001 Dark Nights
Copyright 2019 Elisabeth Naughton
ISBN: 978-1-948050-92-0

Foreword: Copyright 2014 M. J. Rose
Published by Evil Eye Concepts, Incorporated

All rights reserved. No part of this book may be reproduced, scanned, or distributed in any printed or electronic form without permission. Please do not participate in or encourage piracy of copyrighted materials in violation of the author's rights.

This is a work of fiction. Names, places, characters and incidents are the product of the author's imagination and are fictitious. Any resemblance to actual persons, living or dead, events or establishments is solely coincidental.

Acknowledgments from the Author

Special thanks to Liz Berry, MJ Rose, and the entire staff at 1001 Dark Nights who make all of this possible. You support me, you put up with my crazy schedules, and you inspire me every day. Thank you for all you do!

Sign up for the 1001 Dark Nights Newsletter
and be entered to win a Tiffany Key necklace.

There's a contest every month!

Go to www.1001DarkNights.com to subscribe.

As a bonus, all subscribers can download
FIVE FREE exclusive books!

One Thousand and One Dark Nights

Once upon a time, in the future…

*I was a student fascinated with stories and learning.
I studied philosophy, poetry, history, the occult, and
the art and science of love and magic. I had a vast
library at my father's home and collected thousands
of volumes of fantastic tales.*

*I learned all about ancient races and bygone
times. About myths and legends and dreams of all
people through the millennium. And the more I read
the stronger my imagination grew until I discovered
that I was able to travel into the stories… to actually
become part of them.*

*I wish I could say that I listened to my teacher
and respected my gift, as I ought to have. If I had, I
would not be telling you this tale now.
But I was foolhardy and confused, showing off
with bravery.*

*One afternoon, curious about the myth of the
Arabian Nights, I traveled back to ancient Persia to
see for myself if it was true that every day Shahryar
(Persian: شهريار, "king") married a new virgin, and then
sent yesterday's wife to be beheaded. It was written
and I had read, that by the time he met Scheherazade,
the vizier's daughter, he'd killed one thousand
women.*

*Something went wrong with my efforts. I arrived
in the midst of the story and somehow exchanged
places with Scheherazade — a phenomena that had
never occurred before and that still to this day, I
cannot explain.*

*Now I am trapped in that ancient past. I have
taken on Scheherazade's life and the only way I can
protect myself and stay alive is to do what she did to
protect herself and stay alive.*

*Every night the King calls for me and listens as I spin tales.
And when the evening ends and dawn breaks, I stop at a
point that leaves him breathless and yearning for more.
And so the King spares my life for one more day, so that
he might hear the rest of my dark tale.*

*As soon as I finish a story... I begin a new
one... like the one that you, dear reader, have before
you now.*

"Hope is a waking dream."

—Aristotle

Chapter One

Water lapped gently at the shore of the white sand beach, a swish and sigh echoing through the warm night air. High above the pristine coastline, palm fronds rustled, but Zakara's focus was on the surf swirling around her bare feet and the fine sand squishing between her toes.

She'd never been to this beach. She didn't know if it was somewhere in Argolea—the blessed realm created by Zeus for the ancient heroes' ancestors—or if she was somewhere in the human realm. All she knew was that she liked it. She liked how peaceful it was. Liked how breathtaking the scenery was. Liked that here—wherever she'd taken herself this time—no one was telling her what to do or pressuring her to be something she wasn't.

"I'd say you look lost, but something tells me you are exactly where you want to be," a deep male voice said at her back.

Kara whipped around, her long blonde hair blocking her vision before she brushed it aside, and stared at the man reclined on a padded chaise lounge on the beach. A man and chaise that hadn't been there only moments before. A man who was vaguely familiar though she couldn't figure out why.

"I...who are you?" she asked.

"Who do you want me to be?"

His question made her blink. Who did she want him to be? She had no idea. All she knew was that an odd heat was building inside her. One she'd never experienced before.

When he only continued to stare at her, she narrowed her eyes, running her gaze from his thick dark hair down his very muscular body. With his hands clasped behind his neck, his expression expectant, he looked relaxed and just the slightest bit amused. But there was a mysterious glint to his blue-green eyes that belied his stress-free exterior. And though he was gorgeous—tall, dark, and handsome in every way with that chiseled jaw, lush lips, and mesmerizing eyes—something in the back of her mind warned her to be careful.

"Where did you come from?" she asked hesitantly. "We both know you weren't here two seconds ago."

One side of those perfect lips curled. "I'm sure if you concentrate, you'll know exactly where I came from, Zakara."

She didn't like his riddles. And she didn't like that he knew her name when she was still struggling to figure out who he was and why he was so familiar. But the longer he stared at her, the warmer she grew. And as his words circled in her head, it suddenly hit her like a baseball bat right to the forehead.

"You're that guy..." Her eyes grew wide with disbelief. "From my dreams."

He chuckled—a low, deep, captivating sound that was too perfect to be real. "That I am."

He pushed off the chaise—no, pushed wasn't the right way to describe what he did. He all but floated off the damn thing, his beautiful bare feet sinking into the fine sand, the thick muscles in his long legs encased by dark jeans . And as he moved toward her with the thin, white, short-sleeved dress shirt hanging open on both sides, all she could seem to focus on were his chiseled abs and magnificent physique.

"You seem surprised to see me." He stopped in front of her in the surf, the hem of his jeans soaking up the warm water, and gently tipped her face up with one finger. "Though not surprised to be on this beach."

"I..." Kara was having trouble thinking. She *was* surprised to see him. Surprised and elated and *holy-fucking-horny*. But confused as all get out at the very same time. "How...? You came from my dream?"

"Dreams are nothing more than portals to other dimensions. And I didn't come from your dream, *fantasía*. You drew me into your dreams."

He slid his fingers into her hair, and when he leaned down and brushed those lush lips she'd imagined countless times against her temple, she swayed, hypnotized by his heat, his fresh, masculine scent, and that word—*fantasía*...my fantasy—that he'd used to describe her, echoing in her brain.

"Mm..." He skimmed a line of whisper-soft kisses down her cheek toward her ear. "Your skin is as soft as I imagined."

Oh gods... Her eyes slid closed, and tingles rushed over her skin everywhere he touched. He wasn't real. This couldn't be real. She was dreaming again. Losing herself in a fantasy world, her mother would say. But when he moved into her and all his hard perfect muscles brushed against her body, when his warm breath rushed down her neck and he whispered, "I've been waiting for you, *fantasía*," she couldn't seem to stop herself.

Her hands lifted to his chiseled abs as if they had a mind of their own. She turned her face toward his, searching. And almost as if she'd planned it, his lips met hers and opened, drawing her into a spellbinding kiss that curled her bare toes into the sand.

He was wrong. *He* was the fantasy. He knew just how to kiss a woman to make her weak in the knees. He didn't rush things, didn't push her lips open and plunder her mouth. He licked and nibbled until she was breathless for more, and when she opened and drew him in, he took his time tasting and savoring every inch of her mouth as if she were the sweetest wine.

She felt as if she were floating. And maybe she was. Because when she finally pulled back to catch her breath and opened her eyes to look up, she realized she was no longer standing but was laid out on that chaise that had looked only big enough for one before but was now double the size.

She blinked and glanced around. No, it wasn't a chaise anymore. It was a plush, four-poster bed with thin gauzy white fabric hanging from each corner, creating a cocoon right there on the beach.

"You are a delectable treat," he whispered, trailing a hot line of kisses down her throat. "One I can't wait to devour."

Oh gods...his deep voice vibrating from his chest into hers, his silky-soft lips nipping and licking at her skin, his heavenly weight pressing down on her, nudging her legs open...it was all exactly what she wanted, the very scene she'd dreamt of time and again. And too picture-perfect to ignore.

"Wait. This...this can't be possible." She pushed a hand against his chest. "You can't be real. And, and...I don't even know your name."

His hand shifted to the mattress near her head, and he eased back and looked down at her, not the slightest bit irritated or angry that she'd stopped him. "But you do know my name."

She blinked up at his captivating eyes, completely confused by his words. Eyes that weren't just a unique blue-green color as she'd assumed. They swirled with a mixture of blues and greens and purples that seemed to almost sparkle, much like the heavens at night. "I..."

"You know me, *fantasía*. You've always known me." He skimmed his thumb across her bottom lip, his entrancing gaze following the movement until every inch of her body felt alive and tingly. "Say my name and I will take you somewhere you only ever dreamt existed."

He leaned down and brushed his lips against the spot he'd just teased with his thumb. And still confused, she wracked her brain, trying to come up with a name that made sense. But all she could think about was how much she wanted this man—this whatever he was—right this very second. Even if he was a complete stranger. "I..."

His lips slid down her throat again, leaving a line of heat that seared her from the outside in. His weight shifted, and he nudged her legs wider, making room for himself. Unable to fight the sensations he was building inside her, she closed her eyes and thought, *Screw it. It's just a dream. Nothing bad can happen in a dream.*

"Mm, that's it, *fantasía*." His fingers made quick work of the buttons on her blue silky pajama top, flipping them free one by one. Tingles rushed over her skin as cool air met her flesh. "That's exactly what I've been aching for. You. Giving yourself to me freely. Just like this. In a few minutes, you're not even going to care where I take you."

His words were spoken in that same husky timbre, but a shiver of foreboding slid down her spine. And a strange sense that this wasn't just a dream trickled through her. Followed by one that made her feel alive in a way she'd never felt before.

"R-Ryder?"

His lips paused their hypnotic kisses and curled against her overheated skin. "See? You do remember me. Before this night is over, *fantasía*, I plan to hear you scream my name a dozen times from the heavens."

Her breath caught as he went back to nipping at her skin, but it wasn't from fear. It was from the realization that this wasn't a dream. It was real. *He* was real. She just wasn't sure how that could ever be possible.

* * * *

"Well? What news?"

Ryder jerked around at the sound of Zeus's deep voice at his back.

The image of the svelte blonde on the beach faded until there was no more heat beneath him, no more sand around him, nothing but blinding white marble, gilded furnishings, and the perturbed expression of the king of the gods.

He shrugged on his shirt, tugging the two halves together and flicking the buttons through their holes, forcing himself not to think about the female's soft skin and the way she'd felt only seconds ago beneath him. Yes, she'd been hot, but he'd had hot before. And this little interruption was a stark reminder that she was his mark, not his choice. His world didn't mix well with the real world. He'd learned that lesson the hard way. No matter how drawn to the female he was, he knew better than to fall for her. "None. I only just began. And was just as quickly forced to finish because of an asinine question."

"Careful, god."

Ryder wasn't in the mood to be careful. Thanks to Zeus's little interruption, he was going to have to start all over. She'd just let down her guard. Now, the next time he went to her, she'd be on the defensive, wondering why he'd ditched her or—better yet—back to thinking he was a dream. He was no closer to learning anything about the female. No closer to getting the hell out of Olympus and away from the king of the gods. And, thanks to the last ten minutes, horny as freakin' hell. "Try not to take this the wrong way, oh Great King, but you're impatient as fuck."

Zeus flicked Ryder a hard look from across the room with eyes as black as coal. "Let me make something clear to you, dream weaver. You're only here because I've a need for your gifts. And you're only granted leeway in your dealings because of that need. Once you cease to be useful to me and my cause, I've no need to keep you around."

Yeah, Ryder knew that already. Zeus, the god-king of everything, took great joy in lording his dominion over his underlings, every chance he could. He also reveled in reminding all of them—even minor gods like Ryder who didn't normally reside on Olympus—that they could be called into his service at any time.

He checked his contempt, knowing it would do him no good here. Zeus might be an asshat, but he was a powerful one. And though Ryder would like nothing more than to weave a nightmarish hell the king of the gods could never wake from, he knew that was impossible. He'd tried before, failed, and been punished for it. A punishment he was not about to repeat. "We discussed this before. It takes time to build trust, even in a dream world. It's going to take more than one fantasy for this to work."

Forget the fact she'd been pulling him into her dreams for months now. Forget the fact he'd spent those months trying desperately to resist her tempting smile and that luscious body. He didn't want the king of the fucking gods knowing any of *that*. Zeus would only use it against him.

"I want to know if she has the same gifts as her mother."

Ryder frowned. If Zeus had done his homework, he would know the female's mother was a gifted healer. She couldn't see into the past or future as her sisters could do. As descendants of the ancient goddesses the Horae, though, when the three sisters combined their gifts, they were able to see into the present—wherever they chose. Which was the gift Zeus hoped Zakara possessed. A gift Ryder did not want Zeus to get his hands on. "Why don't you just go after the mothers instead of wasting time on a daughter?"

"Because the Horae are carefully protected," Zeus said matter-of-factly. "They rarely leave Argolea and are not easily lured away from those meddling Argonauts."

The Argonauts were the warrior protectors not only of the Argolean realm, but of the human realm as well. And each Horae, coincidentally, was mated to an Argonaut. Once praised by Zeus as heroes—the Argonauts were descendants of the greatest heroes in all of Ancient Greece—now Zeus despised them because they threatened the one thing he wanted most: control over the human realm and all its inhabitants. No god could claim that, though they all wanted it. Sure, Zeus commanded the heavens, Poseidon the seas, and Hades the Underworld, but none could direct the will of man. None could shape the future. And he who could do *that* would be more powerful than all the rest combined.

"The Horae daughters are also ripe for the taking," Zeus went on. "As we saw with the Argolean queen's daughter, they're at that rebellious age where they're desperate to break free of their parents' hold, and anxious for a bit of adventure and romance."

Ryder's blood warmed. Oh yeah, he knew that way too well. Resisting Zakara's advances in her quest for adventure and romance was getting harder and harder for him to do.

Huffing, Ryder reached down for his socks from the marble floor, missing that sand more than he should. "You tend to get love and sex mixed up more often than not. One does not equal the other."

A rare hint of amusement curled one corner of Zeus's lips as Ryder sat on the gilded velvet chaise beside him and pulled on his boots. "Perhaps, but the end result will be the same. With enough seduction, I'll get my answer. And if the female does have any of her mother's or aunts' gifts, it will be easy to lure her out of her hiding place."

That hiding place was Argolea. Ryder still wasn't sure why Zeus just didn't use his own freakin' powers and poof into Argolea to get what he needed himself, but he wasn't about to ask and extend this conversation any longer than it needed to be.

He pushed to his feet and stared the king of the gods down. "I get it. Seduce her, find out what she can do, and report back. We've had this discussion before. Now you're just slowing me down." He moved to step past the god. "If you'll excuse me, I have to weave a whole new world, thanks to your interruption."

Zeus didn't try to stop him, only turned as Ryder headed for the gold double doors in the ugly bedroom suite he'd been given while he was on Olympus, something that looked like King Midas had vomited all over everything. "Hold up, dream weaver."

Ryder paused near the door and glanced over his shoulder.

"Don't get any ideas about the female. She's a means to an end, nothing more."

Ryder's chest tightened. He had plenty of ideas about the female. Ideas that would only put both of their lives in danger. Ideas that were growing stronger and harder to ignore by the day. "Are we done?"

"So long as you remember what's at stake, then yes, we're done."

Ryder's gaze lingered on the god's dark eyes.

His life. Zeus was hinting at Ryder's continued existence.

Thousands of years ago, Zeus had waged war on Ryder's people. The king of the gods had wiped out Ryder's entire family simply because he'd felt he hadn't gotten his way. In the aftermath, Ryder had been imprisoned, and when he'd finally been freed, enslaved. Used not as a messenger as was his original purpose, but as another of Zeus's minions, forced into doing the king of the gods' dirty work. Ryder had no love for any of the Olympians, but as the last surviving dream weaver, he wasn't about to do anything to give Zeus a reason to strike him down. So long as he kept his mouth shut and didn't antagonize the god, he'd be allowed to return home to the heart of the cosmos.

Eventually.

Where no one waited for him. Where no one missed him. Where there was nothing but silence and emptiness.

And where there would never be a sweet, beautiful blonde drawing him into her fantasies, making him the center of her universe.

Motherfucking Zeus. Oh how he despised the god...

"Trust me," Ryder said from between clenched teeth. "I didn't forget. How could I when I've got you here to remind me?"

A slow smile worked its way across Zeus's face. "Very good, dream weaver. You may survive this yet."

Chapter Two

"That should do it," Callia said as Orpheus pushed off the exam table in the medical clinic Kara's mother ran in the Argolean castle. "I would tell you to be more careful when you're out on patrol, but I know neither you nor any of the other Argonauts will listen."

From her spot at the desk in the other room, Kara glanced toward the open exam room door and watched as Orpheus, one of her father's warrior brothers, smirked and tugged down his shirtsleeve over the fresh bandage on his biceps. "Just a flesh wound. Nothing to worry about."

Normally, Orpheus's visits to the clinic entertained Kara and distracted her from the doldrums of her life, but not today. Today she was still on edge from that dream last night. From how real it had felt. From the fact it had vanished as quickly as it had appeared.

"I wouldn't have even bothered you with it," Orpheus said. "But Skyla's been a basket case ever since I had that run-in with the hellhound. And, well, I didn't want to head home and freak her out about this." He was as tall as Kara's father—close to six and a half feet—and just as rugged and muscular as all of the Argonauts. But where her father Zander was blond, Orpheus was dark, and there was always a glint of mischief in his grey eyes that belied the seriousness of his role in their world.

"Smart guardian." Callia pursed her lips. "That was one of your nastier run-ins. None of us were sure you were going to pull through, most of all Skyla."

Skyla was Orpheus's mate, and Zakara remembered all too well the chaos in the clinic the day not more than two weeks ago when the Argonauts had brought Orpheus back from the human realm bruised and bloody and barely even breathing. Or the implication of what a hellhound attack on an Argonaut meant—that Hades was setting something in motion. Something none of them yet knew how to define.

Callia tipped her head, her auburn hair falling over her shoulder as she crossed her arms over her chest. "How are the wounds on your ribs? All healed? Do you want me to take a look at them?"

"No. They're fine." Orpheus reached for his dusty leather jacket from a chair in the corner of the room and tugged it on without even wincing. Looking at him, you'd never know he'd been on death's doorstep only a handful of days ago, but thanks to his superhuman genes, that's how things rolled with the Argonauts. "I gotta get home before Skyla skins me alive. I'm already later than I told her I'd be. I'm sure the kids are driving her batshit crazy right about now."

The kids were Orpheus and Skyla's five-year-old twins—a boy and a girl—both as mischievous as their father. And Skyla was no pushover. As a former Siren—one of Zeus's elite warriors—she could match her mate in any battle. And Kara was pretty sure he was more afraid of her than he was of any hellhound.

Callia laughed and stepped into the reception room as Orpheus did. "Then you'd better get home fast. I don't want to have to close up any more of your wounds tonight."

Orpheus's grin widened. "Thanks, Callia." He looked toward the desk where Kara was finishing her paperwork. "Night, kiddo. Don't let your slave-driver mom here work you too late."

Kara pushed her blonde hair over her shoulder and smiled. "I won't. G'night, Orpheus."

Kara's mother shook her head as she watched Orpheus leave then turned toward her daughter. "Every time one of the Argonauts comes in here all bloody and bruised like that, I'm afraid it's going to be your brother or your father."

Kara was well aware of that fact. Her mother's constant stress over Kara's older brother Max's training with the Argonauts was one of the reasons she wasn't wild about working in the clinic.

She pushed the desk drawer closed and shoved the thought aside as her mother turned back into the exam room. Max was every bit as big and capable as the other Argonauts. Not only that, but with his gift of transference, he was more powerful than the rest of them, able to take on any otherworldly gift of those he encountered. In his late thirties, it was well past time he completed his training with the guardians, but their mother would forever see him as a child. Just as she did Kara. The only difference was, in Max's case, he knew what he was supposed to do with his life. Kara was still searching.

A familiar frustration settled over her, one she didn't like to think about too much, but at twenty-six, it was getting harder to ignore. Her mother was training her to follow in her and her grandmother's footsteps as a healer. But Kara had no interest in treating the injured and sick. And so far, she lacked that one necessary skill for the job—the ability to actually heal anyone with her gift. In fact, *so far*, she had no gift at all.

She moved into the open doorway and leaned against the jamb as she watched her mother tug the bloodied paper cover off the exam table Orpheus had just been sitting on. "I'm finished with the supply lists. Do you need anything else tonight?"

"No, nothing else."

Good, then she could finally get gone. It was already dark outside and she wanted nothing more than to fall into bed and drift into a mindless sleep. "In that case, I'm going to head back to my rooms for the night."

"Kara, wait." Callia tossed the paper in the garbage and stepped toward her daughter. As Kara turned near the door, her mother placed both hands on her shoulders and squeezed gently. "Is everything all right? You've been quiet today."

Kara glanced up at her mother and briefly considered telling her about the weird dream she'd had last night and how real it had seemed, then thought better of it. Her mother would think she was certifiable if she started talking about hunky imaginary men. And truth be told, Kara was starting to fear that already.

That wasn't the first dream she'd had about Ryder. And she desperately didn't want it to be the last. She'd been dreaming about him for months, but last night was the first time she'd actually tasted his lips, felt his hard body against hers, nearly let him slide between...

Her cheeks warmed, and she quickly looked away from her mother. "I'm fine, *matéras*. Just tired. I-I didn't sleep well last night."

"Why not?" From the corner of her eye, Kara saw the way concern creased Callia's smooth forehead. Her mother was several inches taller than Kara, more olive-skinned than pale like Kara, but they shared the same facial features and the same violet eyes. And sometimes, when Kara glanced at her mother, it was like looking at herself in the future. In an alternate future. One in which she had a purpose. "Is something bothering you?"

Sure...the fact that I'm not cut out for this job you think I'm destined for, that I have no gifts like every other Argolean in the freakin' realm, that I'd rather fall asleep and live in my imaginary world with my hunky dream man than exist in this real one...

"No, *matéras*." Again, she worked up that smile that turned her stomach and looked down. "I'm fine. I-I just stayed up too late reading last night."

"Hm." Her mother's lips thinned. She didn't seem convinced, but she let go of Kara and stepped back. "You and your books. Sometimes I think you'd rather spend your life in those books than you would here with us."

Travel to exotic locations? Meet incredible people? Do something amazing and be the hero instead of the bystander for a change? Absolutely those were things Kara wanted. And none of them were in her future because she was stuck in this castle where her parents claimed she was safe, and where nothing exciting ever happened.

None of that was worth mentioning to her mother, however. They'd been around this argument multiple times. After her cousin Elysia had been abducted by Zeus's Sirens and taken to Olympus last year, Kara's parents had been overly protective. They'd nixed Kara's plans to move out of the castle and into a place of her own. They no longer let her leave the castle grounds without some kind of chaperone or armed guard. And traveling? That was a pipe dream at this point since she couldn't remember the last time she'd even been allowed outside the capitol city of Tiyrns' walls.

Argolea was supposed to be a place of peace and prosperity for the great heroes' descendants. A utopia of sorts. More and more lately it felt like a prison to Kara.

To keep from starting another war she knew she'd never win, she turned for her desk in the reception room and reached for her bag. "Okay, then. I'll see you tomorrow."

"Are you sure you don't want to have dinner with us tonight?" her mother called from the other room. "Your father would love to see you. I know he hasn't been around much lately, what with the increase in patrols the Argonauts are running. But he misses you. And Max will be there."

A twinge of guilt tugged at Kara's chest, slowing her steps. She missed her father too, and she'd love to hang out with her brother Max, but tonight she wasn't in the mood to be reminded that she was the one person in their family who didn't have a purpose and who didn't fit in. She just wanted to crawl in bed, forget about the outside world, and fall asleep.

And dream of her mystery man again. Push him back down on that chaise... Straddle his hips... Slide her tongue into his mouth while she let him do whatever naughty things he wanted to do to her body.

"I can't." Her face heated all over again, and she quickly tossed the strap of her bag over her shoulder and told herself fantasizing about a hot guy did not make her nuttier than a pecan pie. "I-I'm meeting Talisa for drinks. Tell *pampas* I miss him too, and I'll try to come see him tomorrow."

"All right." Disappointment sounded in her mother's voice from beyond the open doorway. "Say hello to Talisa for us."

Kara didn't answer. Just made a beeline straight for the stairs and didn't draw a full breath until she was in a different wing of the gigantic castle, several floors up, standing outside her cousin Talisa's door.

Please be home...

She lifted her hand and knocked. For several heartbeats, silence met her ears, then footsteps sounded softly, and the door pulled open to reveal Talisa's familiar smile.

"Hey, you." Dressed in baggy sweats, with her straight dark hair pulled back in a neat tail, Talisa stepped back, allowing Kara to enter her suite of rooms. "I didn't expect to see you tonight."

"I hope I'm not bothering you. I needed an excuse to get out of a family dinner, and, well..."

"Say no more." Talisa smirked as she closed the door at Kara's back. "You want a drink? I was just about to open a bottle of wine."

"Wine sounds heavenly."

"Well, there is a reason they call it the nectar of the gods." Talisa's smile widened as she stepped past Kara. "Come on. You can tell me all about it while we get sloshed."

Kara dropped her bag on a chair in the living room and followed Talisa into a small kitchen. Talisa's suite was similar to Kara's—a small apartment really. But unlike Kara's suite, it wasn't constantly watched, and Talisa was allowed to leave the castle and the city unescorted if she wanted.

That fact burned more than normal as Kara slid onto a stool at the counter and waited while Talisa popped the top on the wine and poured it into glasses. They were the same age—only a couple of months apart—and like their other cousin Elysia, all three of them were linked through their mothers to the ancient Horae, the goddesses of balance and natural order. But even here, Kara was the outlier.

Elysia had proved herself capable after being abducted by the Sirens. She'd even been mated with Cerek, an Argonaut, whom everyone knew could protect her if anything bad happened. And Talisa, though single, was an extremely capable natural warrior herself, being the only female ever born with the Argonaut markings. Kara was the only one of the three anyone seemed to worry about. The only one without a gift. The only one locked in this castle like a prisoner.

"Okay, spill." Talisa handed the glass of red to Kara and leaned against the granite counter. "You are brooding worse than my father."

That tugged a reluctant smirk from Kara as she lifted her wine to her lips. Talisa's father, Theron, was the leader of the Argonauts and the protector of their realm. He had plenty to brood about on a daily basis. All way more important than what was bothering Kara. "That bad, huh?"

"Almost. What's eating at you besides the obvious?"

"The obvious?"

"Your mother, your father, that clinic they've got you strapped to that I know you just *love* spending time in."

Kara frowned and lowered her wine. "If it's so obvious, why can't they tell I hate it?"

"Because they're parents. Parents never notice what we want them to."

Talisa opened a cupboard and pulled out a bowl, which she filled with pretzels and set between them. "If you hate it so much, why don't you just tell them?"

"And do what instead? I'm not qualified for anything else. I have no gifts or skills."

"Still nothing on that front?"

"Not a thing." Kara reached for a pretzel even though she wasn't the least bit hungry. "My mother keeps insisting it will happen, but I'm twenty-six. Max came into his powers before he was even ten."

"True, but that doesn't mean there's anything wrong with you. My mother wasn't able to access her gift of hindsight until she was at least twenty-seven, after she met my father."

"Your mother's a Misos. Her human half was overpowering her Argolean half. It makes sense it took that long for her. I'm not like her. Everyone born and raised in *this* realm comes into their gifts long before their twentieth birthdays, and you know that's true."

Talisa frowned. "Everyone's different, Kara. You have to give it time."

Time was all she'd given it. And time wasn't changing anything. She took a large swig of wine, the sweet red doing nothing to lift her mood.

"What else is eating at you?" Talisa asked.

Leave it to her cousin to see through her walls. "I don't know." She glanced around the living area, itching for...something. "I just feel...restless lately, like there's more to life than this. And I'm really tired of being babysat all the time."

Talisa chuckled. "So tell them that. You're a grown woman. You can do whatever you want."

Kara swiveled back to face her cousin. Even though Talisa was half a foot taller than her and a thousand times stronger, she still managed to look small and feminine standing in baggy sweats in her kitchen. "The way *you've* told them what you want?"

Talisa frowned. "We're not talking about me."

"Have you asked your father again about training with the Argonauts?"

"Not yet."

"Why not?"

"Because he's kind of been dealing with a lot lately, in case you haven't noticed. Hellhounds and conniving gods and injured Argonauts and all that shit. It hasn't been the right time."

"When is the right time?"

"Not right now."

When Kara shot her a look, Talisa sighed and dropped her shoulders. "Gods, we're pathetic. Neither one of us doing what we really want to be doing, neither one able to stand up to our stupid parents. So much for our links to balance and natural order, huh?"

Wasn't that the truth? "The ancient Horae are probably getting a good laugh out of our whining and excuses right about now."

"Touché." Talisa clinked her glass against Kara's. "At least Elysia's got it all figured out. She'll be a kickass queen one day thanks to her time with the Sirens, and she's got a hot hunky hubby now to help her out. One out of three happy endings isn't so bad." She lifted her wine and sipped, but a forlorn expression crossed her violet eyes. One that told Kara Talisa wasn't nearly as confident as she looked.

Kara averted her gaze and sipped her wine as well. Yeah, one out of three of them happy and settled wasn't all that bad. Just as long as you didn't look at how lonely the other two were.

"I've been waiting for you, fantasía…"

Out of nowhere, Ryder's voice filtered through her mind. And she realized her dreams were the one place where she didn't feel less than, where she wasn't restless, where she was never lonely. In her dreams, she knew what she wanted and nothing held her back.

And what she wanted, was him.

She pushed away from the counter and stood. "I have to go."

Talisa's brow lowered. "But you just got here."

"I know. Sorry. I-I just forgot something I have to do."

Talisa followed her into the living room where Kara grabbed her bag from the chair. "What could you possibly have to do at this hour?"

Sleep. She wanted to sleep so she could find Ryder and be that woman she would never be here.

Kara hugged her cousin quickly. "I'll catch up with you tomorrow. Thanks for the wine. And the pep talk. It helped."

Chapter Three

If there was one thing Ryder had learned over the years, it was that dreams were ultimately controlled by the sleeper, not by the weaver. As long as his mark was awake in the real world, he had to wait.

So he'd waited, and planned, and crafted the perfect tropical dreamscape for their next meeting. And when she appeared on the moonlit sandy beach with the gently lapping water against the shore sparkling like a thousand diamonds beneath her bare feet, dressed in nothing but the thin white gown that left very little to his imagination, he was glad he'd waited and planned and woven so intently.

She really was stunning. Every time he saw her he fought the urge to grab her and never let go, something that was completely out of character for him. He wasn't sure why he was so drawn to her. It was more than the fact she kept pulling him into her dreams. It was something else. He sensed a kindred spirit in her. One he hadn't found in anyone else in thousands of years. There was a loneliness to her soul he recognized. A yearning. An emptiness he'd only ever seen in one other person—himself. One he feared they could fill in each other.

It was that recognition that had made him keep his distance. Happily ever after wasn't in his future. Reality and dreams—as he'd learned long ago—did not intermix. It was too dangerous. And he'd spent months successfully avoiding her, only to have Zeus send him straight to her now.

Only now that he was here, some part of him was thankful he no longer had to avoid her. He knew he should go on fighting the attraction but he didn't want to. She was everything he'd been denying himself. Everything he craved. That connection he'd been missing for so damn long. For tonight, at least, he wanted to indulge in the one temptation he knew he could never truly have.

"I wondered when you'd return."

She turned at the sound of his voice and lifted surprised eyes to his. Violet eyes. Mesmerizing eyes. Eyes that softened and warmed the instant they locked on his. "I was tied up all day with family stuff. This was the soonest I could get here."

Damn, he didn't remember those eyes being quite that brilliant.

"Thankfully, you're here now." He reached for her hand, silky soft skin sliding over his much rougher palm, and drew her toward him. Her lithe body brushed up against his without even the slightest hesitation.

"Where is here?" she asked, tipping her face up toward his, teasing him with her plump, pink lips beneath the softly swaying palms in the warm breeze.

"Right where we left off."

He lowered his lips to hers with a kiss that sizzled along every one of his nerve endings and taunted his rock-solid self-control. But before he could deepen the kiss and tease her with the promise of a little pleasure, he registered that the water beneath his feet had turned cold, and the warm breeze that had once been ruffling his hair now left a shiver down his spine.

He drew back, lifted his head, and glanced around the beach, only to gasp at what he saw. No more palm trees, no more powder white sand, no gently lapping waves. The water was now still and black, the shore a mixture of rough sand and small round stones, and there was no more tropical foliage rising from the beach. Instead, steep, rigid mountains stood tall against a starry sky. Mountains covered in pine and fir and spruce and cottonwood.

"What in all the gods..." Still holding her hands, he turned to the left and looked back behind him, no longer seeing his bare footprints in the soft sand as they'd been moments before. Catching nothing but the dark rocky shoreline as it curved around what looked to be a small bay in a rather large lake.

"Something wrong?"

Her sweet voice drew him back around, and he looked down with wide eyes, shocked she didn't seem the slightest bit concerned. "I..."

Words faltered on his lips. Had he altered the dream right there mid-kiss? Subconsciously? If so, that was a first for him. He'd spent meticulous hours weaving that dream so the tropical beach was exactly as it had been the last time they'd met. Females always liked warm, tropical beaches. Nine times out of ten their fantasies took place smack dab in the powdery sand with the water rolling over them. He shaped his dreamscapes around their fantasies even if he never understood the fascination of sand himself. Sand had a tendency to get stuck in places he didn't need it to be stuck. As far as seduction scenes went, he'd much rather have a rustic mountain cabin over a dirty sandy beach any day of the week, but that was never his to choose.

"Ryder?"

He blinked, realizing he'd been staring at her for he didn't know how long. Realizing also that she still didn't look the slightest bit surprised by their change of scenery. And that she hadn't once let go of his hands. They were still warm and solid and soft wrapped around his. "You don't find any of this...odd?"

"Odd?"

"Different?"

Her brow formed the cutest little crease, right between her gemlike eyes. "I'm not sure what you mean."

Yeah, he wasn't sure either. Looking up and around, he realized they were still standing on the rocky mountain lakeshore beach he didn't remember weaving.

Her fingers tightened around his. "It's cold out here. Why don't we go inside and you can tell me what you meant."

"Inside?"

She let go with one hand, stepped past him, and pulled him with her back the way he'd come. Or should have come if he'd ever freakin' been here before. "To the cabin." She smiled and pointed toward the lights on the rocky hillside ahead. "I don't think you brought me all the way out here to freeze, did you?"

Holy hell. He had no idea what he was doing. Or where in Hades *here* even was.

Since she didn't seem the slightest bit concerned with their situation, however, he didn't want to do anything to spook her. So he let her pull him with her down the rocky beach, then up a set of wooden stairs that zigzagged toward a rustic cabin set on a cliff overlooking what was definitely a lake. A big lake, he realized as they climbed higher.

A light illuminated the front porch. She let go of him long enough to reach for the door handle and push it open. Didn't even bother to knock—something else he found odd. But then, she thought this was a dream, one her mind had conjured, so it made sense she wouldn't be worried. He, on the other hand, was freaking the fuck out because he knew how this all worked.

All mortals dreamt. Dreams originated from the subconscious mind. They were rooted in emotions, the strongest of which were centered on a mortal's wants and desires. Mortals could easily conjure their own dreams, but once a dream weaver—like him—arrived on the scene, his powers were strong enough to override anything that mortal could create with her subconscious mind. His dreamscapes were *designed* to override her dreams. Only that clearly wasn't happening now. And for whatever reason, his powers were failing him.

Soft, warm firelight filled the room as he stepped in after her. She shivered and closed the door at his back, then quickly crossed the thick white rug laid out over rustic wood floorboards and stopped in front of the giant stone fireplace to warm her hands by the flames already crackling in the hearth.

A golden glow highlighted her pale skin, the thin cotton nightgown she wore, and made her blonde hair look almost silver in the low light. But instead of being distracted by her sexy silhouette near the flames, he glanced over the rest of the log cabin, hoping it was one from another dreamscape he'd woven. One he'd conveniently forgotten about.

Deep green curtains were already pulled closed at the windows. Comfortable leather couches and dark wood tables filled the space. A rocking chair in the corner of the room. In the corner was a small U-shaped kitchen, and a shadowed open doorway that looked as if it opened to a bedroom or bathroom or he wasn't sure what.

The place was rustic. And cozy. But nowhere he'd ever been and no dreamscape he'd ever conjured.

Without looking toward Zakara, he said, "Stay here."

She glanced over her shoulder but didn't make any move to follow him. Just held her hands out in front of the flames, continuing to warm herself as he headed toward the darkened doorway.

A quick check of the inside and outer surroundings of the cabin revealed it was a small one-bedroom hideaway tucked into a sheltered alcove above the lake. There was no sign of Zeus. And his senses didn't tingle with any kind of warning telling him they were in immediate danger. No indication they were anywhere but in a dreamscape after all. But he still couldn't figure out how he'd woven it. Or when.

He was still working through that one in his head when he came back inside, careful—just in case—to close and lock the door at his back.

"Everything okay?"

He looked up to find Zakara still standing in front of the fire, but this time her back was to the flames, and she was no longer pale or shivering. Her skin was now smooth and soft and relaxed, and her whole body seemed to glow with a warmth that made her ten thousand times more attractive than she'd been before. One that lit a fire deep inside him and heated every space that had just been icy cold with stress and worry.

"Yeah," he said slowly. "Everything's fine." *Still completely freakin' weird, but absolutely fine.*

"Good." A slow smile spread across her lips, and she held a hand out toward him. "Then come over here and sit by the fire with me. You have to be freezing after being outside the last twenty minutes."

Had it been that long? He had no concept of time. But before he could say so, he felt his feet moving as if they had a mind of their own, then her fingers wrapping around his as she drew close and tugged him with her toward the floor.

She sat cross-legged in front of him, the fire at their side, and didn't once let go of his hand. "I have a confession to make."

"You do?"

She nodded. "I've been thinking about being alone with you like this all day."

"You have?"

She nodded again. "The entire time I was with my mother at the clinic, all I could think about was this." She reached for his other hand and closed her warm fingers around his much colder ones. "You."

"What clinic?" Normally, when he had an assignment such as this, he didn't ask questions. Talking was never high on his to-do list in a dreamscape. It was never high on the dreamer's list either. There was really no point. Once he obtained the information he needed from the females who were his targets—and he usually got that through routine seduction—he had no more reason to see them. Certainly had no desire to get to know them. And before things had changed tonight he'd had no intention of talking and getting to know Zakara. But everything seemed different now. He felt different. And he had a strange sense she was the reason his world was suddenly upside down and backward at the moment.

"Oh, it's my mother's clinic. In the castle where we live in Argolea. She's a healer. The queen's personal healer. She services the royal family and any of the Argonauts and their families."

He didn't give a rip about the Argonauts or the Argolean queen. "What do you do there? At your mother's clinic?"

"Nothing really." She rolled her eyes. "Twiddle my thumbs."

Gods, she was adorable. He bet she didn't even know how adorable.

"My mother's training me to be a healer. She thinks I have 'the gift,' like her and her mother before her."

"And you don't?"

She shook her head. "I don't have any gifts."

"What do you mean?"

"I mean..." She glanced down at their joined hands and seemed to contemplate her words. "Geez, I'm not even sure why I'm telling you this." Drawing a deep breath, she looked back up at him in the low light and said, "I'm the only Argolean that I know of who doesn't have any kind of gift."

"None at all?"

"Nope. Nada. Every Argolean has some kind of special ability—strength, intuition, enhanced senses, yadda yadda—bestowed upon them as descendants of the great heroes, but I've got nothing. I'm just"—she lifted her shoulders and dropped them as she looked up at him—"me."

A tingle spread down his spine. She'd just told him exactly what Zeus had sent him to find out. All within the first few minutes of their time together. Without any coaxing on his part or lure of seduction as he'd planned. He could end the dreamscape right now—send her back to sleep in Argolea and him to Olympus with a big fat *so long motherfucker* to the king of the gods. Except...

He wasn't ready to send her home. And he suddenly wasn't thrilled by the idea of returning to his solitary realm in the heart of the cosmos, even though that's all he'd wanted only hours ago.

He swallowed hard, confused yet at the same time eager to know more. His fingers reflexively tightened around hers, as if that would prevent her from getting away. "Maybe you already have your gifts, you just haven't perfected them."

She huffed, but her lips curled, and a sheepish look filled her violet eyes. "Trust me, if I had any kind of gift, I'd know. My mother would know. She is constantly hovering, checking to make sure I'm normal."

He didn't particularly like the sound of that. "Who defines normal? There is no such thing as normal. We're all unique and different. Isn't that the point of life in the first place?"

"I suppose." Her eyes narrowed. "You sound an awful lot like my cousin Talisa."

"I've never met her."

"You'd remember if you had. She's my age, six feet tall, long dark hair, a Siren-shaped body. And she's not at all intimidated by anyone or anything."

"Does she have a gift?"

"Of course. She's the daughter of the leader of the Argonauts. She has the same super-human strength as her father."

"So she could kick my ass? I'll pass, thanks."

Zakara's lips curled into a smile, and she laughed, the sound so light and right and sweet, all he could think about was dragging her onto his lap and devouring it with a kiss so he could feel the vibrations in his own chest.

He resisted the urge, only because he couldn't seem to take his eyes off her. His own lips curled in a smile as he watched a rosiness fill her cheeks. "Confidence in a female is one thing, but knowing a woman is stronger than me might just shatter my ego forever."

She smirked. "I doubt she's stronger than you."

"I'm no Argonaut."

Her gaze swept over his bare shoulders and chest, down his stomach and hovered on his hips and legs crossed in front of him, covered by only the thin linen drawstring pants he'd worn for what'd he'd assumed would be a typical moonlit beach seduction.

Warmth gathered in his groin, and as her gaze slowly lifted back up to his and he saw the flash of approval in her violet eyes, that warmth went white-hot, awakening his cock with an intensity he couldn't quite ever remember feeling before. Superheating his blood with a need that was unlike any other.

"No, you're not," she said in a throaty voice, one he suspected she had no idea made him absolutely on-fucking-fire. "You're more. I'm not entirely sure what you are, but I want to find out. I might not have Talisa's looks or strength or confidence, but all day when I was frustrated with my family and future, all I could think about was coming here and being with you just like this. It was the one thing I wanted with absolute certainty."

Her gaze skipped over his—pure and open and honest—and as he let go of one of her hands and lifted his fingers to her cheek, he was absolutely mesmerized by something—some*one*—who he no longer saw as a target, but as a person who somehow had the power to weave a fantasy around him. "You are a thousand times more confident than you think you are. And strength has nothing to do with muscles. It's found in the soul. Your soul, Zakara, is stronger than you know." His fingers slid down her jaw so his thumb brushed her cheek, and he gently tugged, drawing her forward as he leaned into her, unable to resist the soft, tempting curve of her lips a moment longer. "And as for looks... Your perception *has* to be skewed because I've been all around the cosmos, and I'm here to tell you... You are the most beautiful creature I've ever encountered. Inside and out. There's no way your cousin can hold a candle to you."

"Oh my..."

Her whispered words met his ears a split second before her lips pressed against his. Warmth and softness filled his senses. Then she opened. Her slick, wet tongue slipped against his. Her sweet, hot taste filled his mouth, and he was lost.

His hand wrapped around the back of her head. His other found her hip, the small of her back. He pulled her toward him as he plundered her mouth, and she answered by climbing onto his lap, by trailing her fingers up into his hair, by kissing him so deeply he lost track of who he was and why he was even there.

All he wanted was this. All he needed was more.

All he craved was every fucking thing he hadn't realized he'd been missing each moment of his long, lonely life. Even if somewhere deep inside he knew that a deceitful god like him would never be able to hold on to the gem that was her.

Chapter Four

As far as fantasies went, this one was pretty damn hot. And Kara wasn't about to put an end to it any time soon.

She positioned her knees on the plush white rug on either side of Ryder, gripped his handsome face in her hands, then tipped her head and kissed him deeper as she settled on his lap and the sweet, hard bulge of his erection pressed right where she wanted to feel it.

Ooooh yes...

In the real world, she wouldn't buy into the lines he was hitting her with, but this wasn't the real world. And in this dream, there was no such thing as consequences, so she could be as daring and confident and take-charge as she wanted without having to worry about what anyone would think or say or whisper about her later.

"Mm," he whispered against her lips, his big hands sliding around her backside to cup and pull her into him. "You taste like sin and salvation all at the same time, *fantasía*."

So did he. She gasped as the hard ridge of his arousal brushed her clit. His lips moved to the corner of her mouth, her cheek, worked their way to her throat as he rubbed against her again. Unable to stop the groan building inside her, she closed her eyes and flexed her hips, enjoying the sensation, the electrical arcs shooting all through her body, how wet and tight and achy it was making her.

His fingers fisted the thin cotton of her nightgown at her back and tugged. She answered by pressing her weight onto her knees so he could pull the fabric free between them.

"I want you, Kara." He kissed his way to the other side of her throat, sending a line of shivers all down her spine. "I've wanted you since I first set eyes on you."

Oh, man. He knew just what to say...

Lowering back onto his erection, she looked down into his eyes and shot him a challenging look. "Then why are you wasting time talking?"

Heat flashed in his eyes, and then she was on her back. Soft fur carpet beneath her, hot, hard male looming over her.

He closed his mouth over hers in a possessive kiss that curled her toes against the carpet. But before she could taste her fill and pull him down on top of her, he drew back, his lips trailing across her throat again, his muscular body easing away from her.

"You may regret not putting up a fight." He nipped at her throat, sending a small shot of pain down her spine. But she was too distracted by his knees pushing hers apart. By his fingers tugging the tie at her neckline free. "When I want something, I'm never truly satisfied until I've had all of it. And I want all of you, *fantasía*. Every single part of you. In each and every way imaginable."

Oh, yeeeeessss...

She reached for him as the top of her flimsy nightgown fell open, exposing her breasts. Her nipples puckered as she watched his gaze skip over her, as pleasure filled his eyes.

"Just as perfect as I imagined."

He lowered his head and extended his tongue. Her fingers slid into his hair and her eyes fell shut as she felt the soft, wet flat of his tongue brush across her taut flesh. She pushed her chest out to meet him as he did it again. Couldn't help but press her feet against the carpet and rock her hips upward, searching for the pressure she ached for right between her legs.

"Responsive." He circled the tip, then drew the nub into his mouth and suckled before releasing her. "I like that."

He moved to her other breast, taunting and teasing her nipples into hard peaks, making her hotter and wetter with every stroke of his talented tongue. Kara's whole body was on fire, floating on a fantasy that was better than any she'd ever had before.

"Ryder," she whispered, enjoying every moment, her knees pressing against his ribs as she continued to search for the rest of him. "You're making me wild."

He chuckled and trailed his lips into the hollow between her breasts. "Wild is good." His hot breath fanned her already overheated skin. Reaching down, he grasped the hem of her nightgown at her thigh and tugged up. "Wild is right where I want you."

Cool air washed over her hip, her bare sex, her belly. He pushed her gown higher, past her breasts, and said, "Arms up."

She let go of him long enough for him to tug the gown up and over her head. As he tossed it on the floor beside them, she focused on his face. On the muscle flexing in his jaw as his gaze swept over her naked body, on the approval she saw in his dreamy eyes.

"Oh, I was wrong." He skimmed his thumb down her ribcage, from the base of her breast all the way to apex of her groin. "You're even better than I imagined."

Desire welled inside her. She sat up and reached for his face, drawing him toward her and kissing him deeply the instant their lips met. He groaned into her mouth like a man starved and tangled his tongue with hers, taking charge of the kiss in a way that made her frantic for more. Her hands streaked down the hard plane of his chest and abs until she found the tie at his waist. He kissed her deeper as she pulled it free, shifted his weight on his knees and wriggled out of the garment as soon as she pushed it down his hips.

"I need you now," she mumbled against him, grasping the material with her toes when it was at his ankles so she could kick it away. As soon as it was gone, she wrapped an arm around his waist and another at his neck to pull him down. "I can't wait."

His heavenly weight settled on top of her. The hard, thick length of his cock pressed against her thigh. She wanted to see it, to hold it, to taste it, but his mouth closed over hers again, distracting her from everything but the way he tasted and felt against her.

"I can't wait either." He braced one hand on the carpet and nudged her knees wider as he continued to plunder her mouth with his wicked tongue. His weight shifted. "Need to feel how slick and tight and perfect you are here."

His fingers slid through the wetness between her thighs, and she groaned. But before she could tell him to do it again, the thick, blunt head of his cock pressed against her opening and he flexed his hips, driving deep in one hard thrust.

"Oh, *fuck...*" Her whole body contracted, and her fingertips dug into the damp skin at his lower back as she held on. A mixture of pleasure and pain spiraled straight up her spine and into her brain, mixing with his grunt of pleasure echoing in her ears as he held still so deep inside her she was sure she could feel him everywhere.

He was bigger than she'd expected. Harder. More *real* than she expected from a dream. And though she definitely wanted this—*him*—for a moment she wondered if she'd be able to handle everything he'd implied he wanted to do to her.

His muscles quivered against her hands as he glanced down at her, holding himself still above. "My gods, you're tight."

Her eyes watered as she stared up at the beamed ceiling, willing herself to relax. "And you're...big. Bigger than I expected. I just need—"

"I know exactly what you need, *fantasía*." He shifted one hand between them, drawing his cock back just enough so he could press his thumb against her clit. "Let me show you."

He lowered his mouth back to hers and kissed her deeply, and as his tongue licked against her, he slipped his thumb over her clit, again and again, drawing her passion right back to the surface until any anxiety she'd had moments before was replaced with a burning desire to feel him move.

"Ryder..."

"Yes?"

She arched her back as she kissed him and shifted her hands to his ass, pulling him against her. "Fuck me. Now. I need it. I need you."

He groaned against her lips and drew his hips back. The thick head of his cock dragged along her walls, sending tremors all through her lower body. His thumb continued to tease her clit into a hard nub. And just when she was ready to beg again, he thrust hard once more, filling her so deeply she gasped.

She perched her feet flat on the floor and lifted her hips as he rocked into her again and again, his strokes growing longer with every pass. A fire built inside her. One fueled by lust and desire, the kind she'd only ever read about in books. He lowered his weight onto her and rested his elbow on the floor, tangling his fingers in her hair as he ravaged her mouth. Holding on tightly, she kissed him as passionately as she could, savoring every sensation, the way he was pushing her right to the edge with his magical cock and talented lips, riding the tidal wave of pleasure building inside her.

He tugged his hand from between them and pinched her nipple. Electricity zapped her nerve endings. She gasped into his mouth as he let go of her breast and braced his hand on the carpet, shifting his knees wider and driving harder inside her.

He pulled away from her mouth and stared down at her. Sweat slicked his skin as he plunged deep again and again. His thrusts picked up speed, and a muscle in his neck pulsed with the effort. Her eyes locked on his as the head of his cock, so thick and wide and rigid, hammered into her, striking her G-spot with an almost brutal force. Something primal passed between them, locked in each other like that. Something indescribable. Unable to look away from what seemed to be a swirling cosmos in his eyes, she held his gaze as his hand shifted from her hair to her shoulder, and he closed his fingers around her muscles and bones, pulling her body hard into every one of his savage thrusts.

It was raw. Feral. Animalistic. And hotter than anything she'd ever experienced before. Holding his gaze, she tightened every time he drew back and couldn't keep from groaning when she saw the pleasure in his eyes. When she felt his cock grow even longer and thicker inside her.

The muscles in his face and neck and back grew taut. He shifted his knees higher, shoving her legs up and her feet off the floor as he thrust harder. Deeper. She felt his cock swell to an impossible size inside, one that made her gasp. "Kara...*fuck*..."

Her fingernails scored his sides, and she squeezed everything and threw her head back on the edge of an inferno that was seconds from incinerating her. "There...oh fuck right there don't you dare stop..."

He shoved himself even harder inside her with a series of grunts, and then she felt his whole body contract as he slammed her onto his cock and his orgasm consumed him. His bellow echoed in her ears, but the instant she heard him come, her own release slammed into her, making her blind and deaf to anything but the blistering pleasure exploding outward from her core.

Her rapid breaths were the first things she registered when she came to. Then the sweaty, naked, gloriously perfect male body pressing her into the soft carpet.

"Holy Hera." His warm breath fanned her neck, but he didn't make any move to shift his weight off her, and for that she was glad. He felt amazing against her like this. Warm and perfect against her skin. "What did you do to me?"

She smiled and pressed a kiss to his shoulder, the only part of him she could reach with her lips, as she trailed her hands along his back.

"I'm not sure. Want to do it again?"

He chuckled against her, then slid one hand down her side and shifted just enough so he could roll them both to their sides but still somehow managed to stay locked deep inside her. "You really are a fantasy. And a little vixen. You completely managed to distract me from my plan to seduce you with my fingers and mouth."

"Oh... Well..." She hooked a leg over his hip and shifted closer, drawing him in another inch as she looked up into his eyes. "I had no idea what you had planned. This time I promise not to distract you."

He chuckled again and leaned down to kiss her. "You are most definitely a treat. Why in the name of the gods haven't you already been scooped up by some undeserving male?"

"Because I'm clearly too much for any one man to handle."

His lips curled against hers, and his hand shifted lower, to palm her ass. "You are not too much for me. You are perfect for me."

He brushed his lips against hers, but instead of kissing him back, she eased her head away and looked up into his eyes.

Her chest squeezed tight. "I know this is all just a fantasy, but don't say things like that."

"Why not?"

"Because words—even in a dream—have repercussions. And I don't think I can handle the lasting impact of those words in my real life."

His eyes held hers, but he didn't answer, and she had no idea what he was thinking. She only knew what she was suddenly feeling—a connection to him that wasn't going to help her any in the long run.

Yes, the sex had been hotter than hell and completely amazing, but she *liked* him. Really liked him. More than she probably should. More than she had any man she'd dated or been with before. People back home already thought she lived in her own little world most days. She didn't need to go falling for some imaginary dream guy, because that would only make her want to withdraw even more from society than she already had.

He lifted one hand and brushed a lock of hair away from her cheek. "I know all about the repercussions words have, Zakara. I've avoided certain words my whole life because I've never wanted to deal with those repercussions. You and I are a lot more alike than you know, both playing the avoidance card as much as we can. And I'm definitely not an expert on reality by any means, but I do know this. The only person who controls your reality is you. The only person who can shape it into something meaningful is you. And until you stop worrying about what everyone else wants and thinks and expects from you, you won't own your reality, it'll own you."

His fingers slid into her hair, and he drew her face closer to his. And the intensity she saw in his eyes, the raw truth, shook her to her core and made her heart race hard against her ribs. "But dream, fantasy, or reality...you *are* perfect to me. And I'm not afraid to admit that. You're different from other females I've met. You're honest—maybe because this is the one place you feel free to be honest. I don't know. Whatever the reason, I just know I feel free with you too. More free than I've ever felt before. I'm mesmerized by you, *fantasía*. And I'm not anywhere close to being done with you. Not by a long shot."

He closed his mouth over hers in a blistering kiss. And she opened without hesitation and let him have her, moved by his words, by the feelings they stirred inside her, by the way they made her feel more alive than she ever had when she was awake.

He tugged her on top of him as he rolled to his back, kissing her again and again as she braced knees on each side of his hips and he positioned her just where he wanted her most and started to move.

Pleasure arced through her all over again, shoving aside every worry and neurosis and idiotic fear trying to circle in.

She didn't care if he was going to ruin all men for her in the future. She didn't care if this little fantasy made the real world seem even more meaningless. For one night, she'd savor the fact she was enough—no, not just enough, *perfect*—in someone else's eyes.

And she'd deal with the fallout to her subconscious later.

Chapter Five

Ryder trailed his fingers through Zakara's hair as he lay on his back on the rug in front of the fire. She dozed softly with one leg draped over his and her cheek pressed gently against his chest.

They'd ravished each other twice more there on the floor before he'd finally let her drift to sleep against him, the firelight warming their bare skin. He knew he'd worn her out, but his desire for her wasn't anywhere near slaked, and all he wanted to do was ravage her a fourth time. Yes, he was a god, and yes, he could go all night if he wanted, but this was new for him. Usually—if his seduction scenes went this far, which they rarely did these days—he couldn't wait to finish and get back to his own realm. But with Zakara, things were different. He *felt* different. And he knew that had nothing to do with his libido and everything to do with the fact she'd connected with him on a different level. On an emotional level.

Pressure grew in his chest, an uncomfortable pressure that made him shift beneath her. Emotions—like reality—were not things he had much experience with. They could hinder a god like him. A solitary existence was how he'd survived as long as he had. Yes, it was lonely, but he'd learned long ago that his own dreams—that wanting things himself—only led to trouble. And death.

He glanced down at her relaxed features as she slumbered, remembering the things she'd told him, the brutal truth in her eyes when she'd asked him not to use words that had any lingering repercussions. Oh yes, he knew all about those repercussions. About how words created hope. How hope could lift a person up from the darkest pit, then drop out from under you and leave you shattered against the earth.

After he'd lost his family, he'd avoided any kind of emotional contact for hundreds of years just so he wouldn't have to deal with those repercussions. But he was tired of doing that. He was tired of doing and being what everyone else wanted and expected. And, by gods, he was tired of being alone.

That pressure condensed until a sharp pain stabbed right in the center of his chest, one that nearly made him gasp. He closed his eyes and tried to breathe through it. And then it popped, sending ripples of relief through every cell in his body.

Staying here with Zakara was stupid. And reckless. And he was most likely going to regret this night and everything he'd let happen. But he didn't care.

This felt right. This felt real. This made him feel alive. And it had been so damn long since he'd been alive, he couldn't hold back.

He rolled Zakara to her back and softly brushed his thumb against her cheek. "*Fantasía?*"

She didn't open her eyes, so he skimmed his knuckles across her cheek again, marveling at the fact she really was his fantasy woman. He'd called her that from the start without even realizing he was doing so. He never used cutesy nicknames with his marks. Then again, he'd never met a mark like her.

"*Fantasía?*" he whispered again. "You're not sleeping, are you?"

She still didn't open her eyes, but she smiled as he touched her, then slid her hands up his arms as if she couldn't get enough of him either.

Relief rippled through him. Snoozing was one thing. Falling into a deep sleep might send her back to the real world. Normally, he controlled when his marks entered and left his dreamscapes, but this wasn't a dream world he'd woven, and nothing about tonight was normal. He wasn't ready to let her fall asleep and possibly leave him. Not when he wasn't anywhere close to done with her.

He dropped his head and kissed her shoulder, her collar bone, slowly worked his lips up her throat as he nudged her knees apart and climbed between her legs, already hard and aching for the slick, wet heat he knew could drive him to a blinding release. "I have to have you again. I know you're tired, but I just can't help myself. You're too tempting lying there all soft and sexy and perfect."

She sighed again and let her legs fall open wider, making room for him between her thighs, right where he ached to be. "Mm..." Her fingers slid over his arms, down his shoulders and along his back as she arched her back and lifted her hips to meet him. "Then have me. I'm yours."

I'm yours...

If only she could be. He pushed deep inside her, savoring her pleasure-filled sigh echoing in his ears.

Oh yes, he was going to regret this night. He was going to regret it for a very long time. So he had every intention of enjoying every damn minute they had left.

* * * *

Kara rolled to her back and stretched in the warm sunlight sliding over her. She'd had the most delicious dream, one that had felt so real she could still feel the lingering pleasure all through her body.

She didn't want to get up—it was Saturday so she didn't have to be anywhere today—but the bright light was too insistent and she knew she wouldn't be able to sleep any longer. Deciding she'd make a cup of tea and dive into her latest book, she opened her eyes and blinked several times as the ceiling came into view.

Wood slats. Darker wooden beams. Confusion trickled through her mind as she stared up, wondering why the ceiling in her suite was no longer white and edged with fancy molding.

She suddenly became aware of something soft and furry beneath her bare back, covering something harder than her mattress below that. Glancing to the left, she spotted a large stone fireplace filled with glowing embers from a recent fire, and to the right—she held up a hand to block the bright glare—large picture windows that looked out over a glimmering lake.

Her eyes flew wide, and she bolted upright, stumbling as her feet got caught in the blanket pooling at her ankles. Cool air whooshed over her, sending a shiver down her spine, and she scrambled for the blanket and quickly pulled it around her naked body.

She turned a slow circle, taking in the log walls, the leather furnishings, the small kitchen across the space. Her heart beat hard and fast. She had no idea how she'd gotten here or where *here* even was, but one thing was clear: this was the cabin from her dream. Her wide-eyed gaze darted down to the white fur rug beneath her bare feet. That was the rug where her fantasy man had ravished her. Either she was still sound asleep in the midst of that dream, or none of what had happened was a fantasy, and all of it was re—

"It can't be real." Her pulse was a whir in her ears as she shoved the blanket back from her arm with shaking fingers, grasped the skin of her forearm between her thumb and first finger, and pinched down hard.

"*Skata.*" Pain shot all across her arm and up into her shoulder, making her gasp, but her surroundings didn't change. She was still in the small cabin. Still completely naked. Still alone, though she had no fucking clue how any of this was even possible.

"Okay, think, Kara," she mumbled to herself. Her mind spun as she breathed slowly so as not to hyperventilate. If she wasn't asleep, that meant this was definitely real. And if the cabin was real, then she was outside the walls of Tiyrns.

Her stomach tightened. That wasn't exactly good news. Yes, she hated being locked up there like a prisoner, but she understood why her parents were so cautious. Elysia had been outside the castle walls when Zeus's Sirens had abducted her and taken her to Olympus.

Swallowing hard, she grasped the blanket tighter and glanced around the cabin again, trying to remember if she'd ever been here. Nothing seemed familiar, at least not from before last night. Her gaze darted to the windows and the shimmering water beyond. The lake or sea or whatever this cabin overlooked was big. Steep, white-capped mountains edged the water on three sides, but she couldn't see any land in the distance. She could be in a cabin perched over the Tyrrenhian Sea in the northern region of Argolea. That would explain the cold and snow this time of year. If so, she wasn't far from the port city of Heraklea, though her parents would flip the fuck out if they discovered she'd traveled so far from home.

Had she flashed here? Argoleans could travel great distances via teleportation in their own realm. She didn't remember flashing. She didn't remember anything but that scorching hot dream. Her gaze darted back down to the white fur rug, and the image of herself there on her back, naked and moaning and arching up against Ryder's sinful body as he ravaged her, burned through her brain and set fire to her cheeks.

"A dream. It was just a dream..." Mortified, she rushed toward the open bedroom door. A tidy bed and two side tables filled the space. Across the room, another door opened to a bathroom.

She swept into the bathroom, ignoring her haggard reflection in the mirror, flipped the faucet on, then bent over and splashed cool water all over her face. The liquid sliding down her skin helped chill her out, but as she turned the water off, she suddenly became aware of another kind of wetness. This one between her legs.

Her eyes grew wide. Her hands shook as she quickly wrestled the blanket open. One look was all she needed to know she'd had sex. A lot of sex.

"Oh my gods..."

Real. Last night had been *real*. Not a dream. Not a fantasy. Not a figment of her imagination. It had been completely fucking real.

He had been real.

Her heart raced. Her mind spun. Thoughts—consequences—zipped around in her brain. She had no idea where Ryder had gone or if she'd ever see him again, but she didn't care. Right now, the only thing that mattered was getting home. She wasn't a warrior like her cousin Talisa. She had no combat training like her other cousin Elysia. She had no gifts whatsoever she could use if she found herself in danger. She understood now why her parents didn't want her venturing outside the walls of Tiyrns alone. Because it wasn't safe. And she wasn't stupid enough to stay here and test fate when common sense was telling her flashing home as soon as possible was the smartest choice she could make.

Of course, flashing back to the castle in nothing but a blanket or her thin nightgown—wherever it was—wasn't a bright idea. It was broad daylight. Since she couldn't flash through walls, any of the guards or Argonauts or—gods forbid—her family could inevitably run into her. Moving to the closet at her right, she pulled the doors open and scanned the few items of clothing on the shelves. They were mostly men's, but she figured they'd work.

She dropped the blanket at her feet and grasped the smallest pair of pants she could find. They were easily three sizes too big, but she gathered the waistband and cinched it tight with a belt. After tugging on a blue checked flannel shirt, she rolled the sleeves up to her elbows and stuffed the front tails into her baggy pants. A quick scan of the closet floor told her there were no shoes, but she could deal with being barefoot. At least she was no longer naked.

Raking her fingers through her hair, she pushed it back from her face and turned back into the living room, intent on heading outside so she could flash back to Tiyrns. Halfway to the door, she spotted her nightgown on the floor, and a thought hit, stilling her steps once more on the furry white rug in front of the fireplace.

What if she wasn't in Argolea? What if Ryder or whoever he really was had taken her to the human realm? Her heart raced all over again. She wasn't an Argonaut. She couldn't open a portal back to Argolea on her own. If he'd somehow invaded her dream or hypnotized her so he could abduct her and take her to the human world, she really was in danger.

The door swung open in front of her. She gasped and jerked back. Then focused on Ryder—the man who'd just turned her world upside down in every way possible—as he stepped into the room barefoot, wearing those low-riding linen pants she remembered from last night and a heavy red flannel shirt he had to have gotten from that closet.

"You're awake." He closed the door at his back and smiled down at her, his dark hair rumpled, his cheeks rosy from the cold, a sexy layer of scruff on his jaw making him look drop-dead gorgeous in the early morning light. "I thought you'd sleep awhile longer."

"I..." Holy hell, her brain was complete mush. She willed herself to step away from him, but her legs didn't seem to want to listen. The scents of leather and pine with just a hint of citrus surrounded him as he moved toward her, making her whole body melt with the remembered feel of his fragrant skin rubbing up against hers.

"I couldn't sleep so I went for a walk. I didn't want to wake you." He reached for her arms, gently tugging her close as he ran his hands up and down her tight muscles, then leaned down and softly kissed her.

Her head grew light. She lifted her lips to his without even realizing she was doing so and sighed as his mouth brushed hers. He drew back and smiled down at her, still massaging her arms, still as blindingly beautiful as the sun. And as she blinked up at him and tried to tell herself he was a stranger, that she should be wary and cautious and smart, she realized...she didn't want to be any of those things. She wanted him. Here, now, all over again. She didn't care about the consequences.

Something in his eyes heated, and he leaned down and whispered, "I want you again too," just before he kissed her once more. Only this kiss wasn't soft and gentle and chaste. It was wet and erotic and demanding, and it burned through her entire body like molten lava on the move.

She was breathless when he drew away from her lips. Fuzzy-headed when he squeezed her arms and said, "But first we need to talk."

"T-talk?" Holy Hades, what was this man doing to her? "About what?"

"This." He let go of her with one hand and raked his fingers through his hair. "I think I have it figured out. It's unconventional but I think it will work. Do you want tea? I didn't find coffee in the kitchen but I think there's tea."

Confused, she turned as he stepped past her and moved into the kitchen, filling a kettle with water and setting it on the stove. "Ryder, what's going on?" Now that his heat and scent and sexy touch weren't distracting her, she could think again. "And where are we? I don't recognize this place."

"I don't either. I was kind of hoping you knew."

"Why would I know? You brought us here."

"Actually, I didn't." He pulled a canister from the cupboard and set it on the counter next to the stove. "I took us to that tropical beach. You brought us here."

"What?" That made absolutely no sense. "No, I didn—"

He moved back in front of her. "You changed the dreamscape. You made it real."

Real...

She glanced around the cabin, her mind spinning. She'd sensed it was real only moments ago, and now he was confirming it for her. Her pulse picked up speed. "But I... I can't—"

"Apparently you can. Pretty cool gift, if you ask me. One I didn't expect when I went to find you."

She had no idea what he was babbling about. All she could focus on was the fact she'd somehow shifted a dream into reality.

And Holy Hades...the implications of *that* were too numerous to even comprehend. The blood drained from her face as she stumbled back a half step. She never would have done the things she'd done last night if she'd thought any of it was real.

"Now listen." He moved closer and gripped her upper arms. "I'm going to have to run a quick errand before we leave. It shouldn't take long, but it's important. Once I'm back we can head to my place and pick up where we left off. It's not what you're used to, but I think you're going to like it."

Skata, she was having trouble focusing. "Your...place? In Argolea?"

"No, not in Argolea. My home's far away. In the center of the cosmos. Outsiders aren't usually allowed in, but I can protect you there. Keep you safe." He moved even closer, his body brushing hers and his scent swirling around her. "And we can be together there with no one telling us who to be or what to do or how to act."

Nothing he was saying made sense. Except for the fact he didn't live in Argolea. "I... You want me to run away with you? We barely know each other."

"You know me." He brushed his knuckles down her cheek, leaving a line of heat in their wake. "You've been drawing me into your dreams for years, only I was such a stupid fool I resisted. I shouldn't have done that. I should have made you mine years ago."

Dreams. The center of the cosmos. Safe... Those weren't normal words.

She looked up into his eyes, a warning tingle rushing down her spine. "Who are you? If you're not Argolean, then you're either human or..."

Her words faltered as he stared down at her. And in the silence it hit her, sending her a step away from him. "You... You're a god." Her chest seized. "From Olympus?"

"No." He moved close once more and reached for her hand, preventing her from stepping further away. "I'm not from Olympus. I promise you that."

She tried to pull her hand free, but he closed his fingers tightly around hers. "Don't tou—"

"I'm not like the Olympians, and I'd never do anything to harm you. I wouldn't even be here if it weren't for you."

She tried again to pull free but his hold was too strong. "What the heck does that mean?"

"It's hard to explain. Complicated."

She wasn't buying that. Her eyes widened. "Well, try. Because I'm not going anywhere until you do."

He sighed. "Okay, just...try to keep an open mind." His gaze met hers. "I'm what the Olympians consider a cosmic deity. I can exist in mortal realms, but I spend most of my time in the dream world. That's where we met. A long time ago. You pulled me into a dream you'd conjured, and I was tempted by you, but I learned long ago that mixing dreams with reality rarely ends well. At least for those from my line. You see, thousands of years ago, the Olympians lured my family out of the dream world and into reality. And that's when Zeus destroyed them."

"All of them?"

"Every single one but me. I was... I was away at the time. They were all killed. And I...I couldn't help them." He glanced away and then looked back at her. "I'm the last. I've spent every day since making sure I don't fall to the same fate so my line lives on. And when you started pulling me into your dreams, I was attracted to you, and clearly tempted, but I was able to keep my distance. Until last night."

She felt herself falling under his spell all over again. Growing weak at the way he was caressing her hand. Going soft at the intense look in his eyes as he gazed down at her as if she were the only thing he could see. "W-what was so different about last night?"

"*You* were different. You were confident and strong, and you had a plan I couldn't compete with. Make no mistake, I had every intention of sending you back to sleep, just as I've always done when you've drawn me into your dreams, but you changed my plans. You changed the dreamscape. You made it real. You brought us here and rocked my entire world, and now"—he reached for her other hand, lifted both and pressed his lips to each, one by one—"now I don't want to send you back to sleep. Now I don't want to leave without you. Now, I just want more of you. More of what we had last night. More of us and this feeling inside me."

She stared wide-eyed up at him, confused and anxious and— dammit—completely awed by the tenderness in his gaze. "W-what feeling?"

His lips curled in a sexy smile. "Alive. You make me feel alive, *fantasía*. Alive and whole and real. And those are things I haven't felt in a very long time. Since before I lost my family. I didn't plan this any more than you did. I didn't want it. But now that it's happened...I can't go back to pretending as I did before."

He let go with one hand, wrapped his arm around her back, and drew her into the heat and life of his body as he brushed his lips against her temple, hypnotizing her with the sound of his voice. "The repercussions can be damned as far as I'm concerned. I want you and this and us. You told me you were mine last night, and you are. You're

mine and no one else's, and I'm not giving you up. Come home with me. I promise you won't regret it."

Oh, he felt heavenly as he pulled her closer. His words were like poetry, everything she'd dreamt of hearing from a man who adored her. And when he kissed her...it was like tasting the sweetest wine. But something wasn't right. She still had no clue who he really was or what was actually going on. And as much as she longed for adventure and passion and something different in her life...this wasn't it.

"No." She shifted her arms to his chest and pushed against him, breaking the kiss that could so easily sway her will and buckle her knees. "No, stop. I can't."

"Zakara—"

"No." She stumbled back a step, thankful and surprised he'd released her. "This is insane."

"Insane would be ignoring what's happening between us."

"Happening? Nothing's happening." She moved another step away, a rising panic growing inside her. One she didn't understand and couldn't seem to stop. "All that happened was I let you fuck me. And I only did that because I thought you were a dream."

"Zakara." He reached for her again but she shot to the side, out of his reach.

"No, don't. Oh my gods, this is nuts. *You* are nuts. I must be nuts for even listening to all this." She pressed a hand against her abdomen. "And after one crazy night you want me to go home with you? To the cosmos?" A hysterical laugh got stuck in her throat. "I have a family. I have friends. I have a life in Argolea. I can't just drop all that and run off with you when I don't even know anything about you."

"Why not?"

"Why not?"

He stepped toward her and grasped her hand before she could pull it away. "You yourself told me you don't fit in with that life in Argolea."

"That doesn't matter. It's—"

He stepped toward her. "You told me you feel like an outsider there." He brought her knuckles to his lips and gently kissed her skin again. "You're not an outsider with me. You fit perfectly with me. And you do know me. You've known me for a very long time. If you didn't, you never would have come here with me. You're not a reckless girl, Zakara. You came here because you trusted me. And you made love with me all night long because you felt the same connection I feel every time I look at you. That's not crazy. That's not insanity. That's real. Reality is simple if you think about it. It means being true to yourself. To who you are and what you want to be. And being true can set you free. I'm free in my world, *fantasía*. You can be free there as well. You can be free with me."

She stared up at him, mesmerized by the swirling colors in his eyes, searching his gaze for any sense that his words were true. What she saw was a tender honesty that pierced her heart and awakened some long-sleeping part of her she didn't know existed. He believed everything he was saying. He truly wanted her. He was everything she'd fantasized about all these years, standing in front of her, offering her things she'd only dreamed of.

"I..."

"Say yes, Zakara." He eased in closer and brushed his sinful lips across her temple, hypnotizing her all over again with his words and heat and seductive scent. "Say yes and come with me."

Come with me...

Could she? Could she leave her family? Her eyes drifted closed as he pressed his lips down her cheek, a shiver following the heat of his mouth. Could she run away with him like that? Abandon everything and everyone? She wasn't sure, but oh, she suddenly wanted to. She longed to live her life the way *she* wanted, not the way others experienced. Ached to experience adventure. Passion. Freedom. To be the hero of her own story. And he was offering all of that to her. The chance to truly be *alive* instead of asleep as she'd felt all these years. And he was offering himself. Her fantasy man brought to life.

Yes... She wanted all of that. Turning her head so she could find his lips, she lifted her hands to his chest and opened the moment his mouth closed over hers.

Yes, yes, yes... She wanted him. She wanted everything.

The door to the cabin burst open, breaking the spell. Startled, Zakara jerked back from Ryder's mouth and whipped around to stare wide-eyed at the three female warriors dressed in boots, leggings, and curve-molding tops, their long hair blowing in the slight breeze behind them, each with a bow and arrow aimed right at her heart.

Sirens. *Oh gods...*

Every muscle in her body went rigid with terror.

"Hello, Horae," the one on the right said.

At her back, Ryder's big hands closed over her arms and held tight.

"Nice work, dream weaver," the Siren on the left said, stepping further into the room, her arrow still poised for release. "It was smart of you to keep her from fleeing before we could arrive. But now it's time to take her back to Olympus."

Chapter Six

Panic wrapped like a boa constrictor around Ryder's chest as the closest Siren to Zakara reached out and jerked her away from him. "The king of the gods is waiting, little one. Let's finish this, shall we?"

If he let her out of his sight, he knew he'd never see her again. "Hold on—"

"Your job here is done, dream weaver," the blonde Siren in the middle said, glaring over Zakara's head toward him. "You're free to return to the cosmos."

Zakara turned shocked eyes his way as the Sirens tugged her toward the door. Shocked and bitterly betrayed eyes. Eyes he had to ignore if he was going to get them out of this.

He looked past Zakara and focused on the Siren. "Zeus is waiting for my report on her Horae abilities."

"We can fill him in."

"And what are you going to tell him? You know nothing."

The Siren's jaw clenched down hard. At her side, the redhead lowered her bow and whispered, "He's right. Let him report back what he knows. If Zeus isn't satisfied, he'll punish the dream weaver. If he is, he'll send the dream weaver on his way. Neither are our concerns. We were only sent to get the girl after he lured her into the human realm."

Zakara's eyes narrowed with blistering anger, but Ryder continued to ignore her. Her only chance now was for him to play along. And for him to find a way to somehow convince the king of the gods she was useless.

"Fine," the blonde said. "Bring them both. Zeus is waiting."

The redhead grasped his arm and tugged him toward the door

behind Zakara. She grunted and stumbled but he didn't have a chance to check to see if she was all right. By the time he stepped foot on the front porch of the small cabin, she was already gone, flashing to Olympus. That panic seized his chest all over again, but he forced himself to remain calm and let the Siren at his side open her own portal.

Light flashed, and he felt himself flying. And then ground solidified under his feet, and he looked up to see the familiar yet stomach-churning view of Olympus—ornate marble and gold temples, towering fountains, and immortals of all kinds milling about, doing nothing but eating and drinking and feasting over their successes.

"This way." The redhead dragged him forward, toward the biggest and most elaborate temple at the end of the street. The one dripping with gold that stretched into the sky.

Zeus's temple always turned Ryder's stomach. There wasn't a single thing beautiful or relaxing about it. A large hall with towering columns greeted him. A long rectangular pool took up most of the floor space in the center. At the end, on an enormous raised dais, the king of the gods lounged in his opulent chair, looking bored as he waited for the Sirens to haul Zakara and Ryder to a stop at his feet.

He was old, thousands of years old, but you'd never know by looking. Zeus was the epitome of the perfect male specimen—tall, muscular, dark—with chiseled good looks, a human in the prime of his life who didn't look a day over thirty-five. But he wasn't perfect. And he wasn't human. And as he pushed out of his gilded chair and rose to his full height at over seven feet, Ryder was reminded just how powerful the god really was. What he could do to those who crossed him. And the games he liked to play with the underlings he kept at his beck and call.

"Well now, dream weaver. It seems you brought me a prize."

Zakara didn't speak. Just stared up at the king of the gods with wide eyes as he moved slowly down the marble steps, almost as if she couldn't believe what she was seeing.

Ryder held his breath and silently cursed himself for not forcing her to go to the cosmos with him sooner. For wasting time going for a walk this morning to sort things out in his head. If he'd stayed with her, if he'd convinced her to leave with him earlier, she wouldn't be here now. Zeus wouldn't have her. The king of the gods wouldn't have possession of one of the Horae descendents—the ancient goddesses of balance and justice. Ryder still didn't know if Zakara had any untapped Horae powers, but if she did, Zeus would find them. And if that happened, she wouldn't just be in danger, those in her realm, those in *every* realm would be in jeopardy.

Zeus stopped in front of her, tipped his head, and let his gaze wash over her. "Pretty little thing, isn't she? Odd choice of clothing, but I'm sure we can find something a little more appropriate."

He glanced to his left, where a servant girl dressed in a white toga stood waiting. "Find our guest something more suitable to wear. And have a room prepared."

"Yes, my king." The servant girl bowed, then quickly rushed from the room.

Zeus made a slow circle around Zakara, then stopped in front of her once more. "Definitely pretty. Prettier than her cousin, I must say. What do you think, Morpheus?"

Ryder chanced one look at Zakara. She didn't glance his way, but he saw the way her shoulders stiffened at the use of his formal name. "I wouldn't know, my king. I never met the cousin."

"Elysia was definitely a looker. Would have been better with some of my adjustments, had she stayed with the Sirens, but this one doesn't need any of those. Tell me, girl. What's your name?"

Zakara didn't answer. Only continued to stare up at the god.

Zeus looked Ryder's way. "Is she mute?"

"No. I think just shocked. Her name's Zakara."

"After her father, the Argonaut Zander, no doubt." Zeus looked back at Zakara. "Pity she won't be seeing her father for a good long while. I'm sure that'll piss off those meddling Argonauts."

Zakara's mouth fell open as Zeus moved away from her and stepped in front of Ryder. "You have something to report?"

Shit. Here they went...

Ryder worked to keep his shoulders relaxed. "I do. She has no Horae powers. She can't see into the future, past, or the present."

The glare Zakara shot his way could have melted ice, but Ryder ignored it and stayed focused on Zeus.

"You're sure of this?" Zeus asked.

"Completely. She's of no use to you."

Zeus's eyes narrowed, and a tingle rushed down Ryder's spine at the assessment he saw in the god's eyes. "Perhaps not," Zeus finally said. "But I've decided to keep her just the same. Khloe?"

The king of the gods turned away. The redheaded Siren stepped forward once more. "Yes, my king."

"Take Zakara here to her room. See that she's properly bathed and dressed. Then bring her to me in the grotto. We've much to discuss."

Oh no... Ryder stepped toward Zeus. "But—"

"Your obligation to me is fulfilled, dream weaver." Zeus held out a hand, and an arc of electricity shot forward, surrounding Ryder in a halo of energy that stilled his feet and left him immobile. "Return to the cosmos. If I need you again, I know where to find you."

Zeus threw his other hand forward, and the power that slammed into Ryder sent him spinning through time and space until there was nothing but darkness.

* * * *

"I don't know! I've told you multiple times I don't know. It's the truth. I swear it!" Kara chanced a look at the king of the gods from her spot on the marble bench in the middle of the elaborate grotto. He didn't believe her. Even after she'd answered every one of his questions and been brutally honest about what had happened in that cabin, he didn't believe her. And she wasn't sure what to tell him to make him *see* she wasn't lying.

"I know the dream weaver did not take you to the human realm. It's beyond his powers. You altered the dream he created and morphed it into reality. You have to be the one who transported you both there."

There was no way that was possible. And she was still too shaken over the fact Ryder was Morpheus, the god of dreams, and that he'd tricked her all on Zeus's orders to think too much about that fact. "It wasn't me. That's what I've been trying to tell you. I don't have any powers."

"You lie. All Argoleans have some kind of gift. I bestowed that upon the heroes' ancestors when I created the realm of Argolea."

"Well, you messed up with me because I'm not like anyone else in Argolea. Ask anyone who knows me. They'll tell you the same thing. I've no gifts or powers at all. There's no way I could make a dream into reality. I can barely take care of myself let alone someone or something else."

Zeus stopped in front of her, his jaw locked tight, his eyes hard and unfriendly. "You test my patience, female."

She could tell. Not that she was trying to test him—she didn't want to do anything to piss the god off. She just wanted to get the hell out of here. But her inability to do or be what someone else expected was again biting her in the ass, making her feel like a monumental failure.

"I'm sorry. If I knew how to help you, I would." *Lie.* "I just...don't." She curled her fingers into the stone bench and chanced another look up at him. "Can I please go home now?"

"You are home." He glanced to the left. "Guard."

A male who was as big as one of the Argonauts and dressed in some kind of armor stepped out of the shadows of the plants in the grotto.

"I'm done with her for now."

"Yes, my king. Shall I take her back to her room?"

Her "room" had been as plush as any hotel suite, with a big four-poster bed, marble bath, and a stone balcony that looked out over the view of Olympus. The Grecian peach gown they'd made her dress in she could do without, but the room had been nice, and she was suddenly so tired, all she wanted was to fall asleep on that big bed and deal with reality later.

"No." Zeus pinned her with a hard look. "If she's not going to cooperate, neither will we. Take her to the pit."

Shock rippled over the guard's face as he looked from Zeus down to Zakara and back again. "Y-yes, my king."

Her stomach tightened with fear as the guard grasped her by the biceps and pulled her from the bench. Zakara had no idea what was going on, but as she was led toward the arched opening to the grotto, Zeus's voice stopped her.

She glanced over her shoulder, a tremor of terror rushing down her spine at the malice she saw in the king of the gods' soulless black eyes.

"I can be your greatest savior or your worst nightmare, female. Think long and hard about that fact before our next meeting."

Chapter Seven

His skin was stretched so tight across his chest, Ryder was afraid it might rip in two.

Starlight sparkled all around him as he stood in the center of his homeland, Oneiroi, the wavering blues, greens, and purples of the cosmos illuminating the clouds beneath his feet and the ether surrounding him. Breathing deeply, he turned a slow circle and scanned the mountains and trees, the shimmering waterfall that fell into the mystical pool of Lethe, the arched rock opening beyond that led to his private retreat.

Once, he'd lived here with his family, until Zeus had destroyed that dream. Hours ago, he'd envisioned living here with Zakara, but Zeus was once again invading his world, twisting what should be a fantasy into a blistering nightmare.

He wasn't going to let the king of the gods win this time. Not when he had the power to stop him.

Thoughts tumbled through his mind. He wasn't sure how Zeus's Sirens had found them, but they'd mentioned the human realm when they'd come for Zakara. He knew for certain he hadn't morphed their dreamscape into reality, which meant she had. She had a gift she didn't even realize she could control, and that was what Zeus wanted, he realized. The ability to shift dream to reality had lingering repercussions. If she perfected that gift in a wakeful state, Zeus could manipulate her to his advantage whenever he wanted. He could, in effect, alter reality in ways that wouldn't just be dangerous for any mortals or immortals in his way, they could be downright detrimental for the whole of mankind.

Urgency and a need to stop Zeus, to save Zakara, caused his chest to tighten even more. He would never get back to Olympus without Zeus knowing. He needed someone to act as a diversion. He was a loner, though. He existed in this realm entirely by himself. He had no allies. His only living relatives—his grandmother Nyx, the shadowy goddess of night, and Thanatos, the barbarian god of death—were not entities he could go to for help. If they learned of Zakara's gift, they'd each want it for themselves.

No, he had to turn to someone else, but who?

His conversation with Zakara the night before filtered through his mind, and in a heartbeat, he knew.

He rushed past the waterfall and into his cave, quickly locating the magical powder his father Hypnos had left. Grabbing a vial of the glittering substance, he shoved it in his pocket and headed for the door. Once back out in the shimmering colors of the cosmos, he closed his eyes and imagined the female who was his new target.

Thankfully, she was still asleep. She hadn't risen for the day, was sleeping in on her weekend, which meant he had time to make this work.

He didn't bother weaving a dreamy beach scene as he'd done in the past. She was already in the midst of her own dream, he found. A nightmare to some. A fantasy to her, he realized. And the male who was with her...

Holy fuck...that was not a male he wanted any part of.

Her long black hair flew all around her as she swiveled, ducked under the male's blade, then swung out with her own weapon. Perspiration dotted her forehead. Metal clanked against metal, and grunts filled the night air as they battled across the ridge. Ryder's adrenaline surged as he stood in the shadows of the forest and waited, wondering what the hell kind of dream this was and why she was conjuring a battle with the Prince of Darkness, Hades's depraved son, but her twisted fantasies were not his concern. His only concern was getting to Zakara and making sure Zeus didn't harm her.

It nearly killed him, but he waited until Talisa got the upper hand in the battle. As soon as she shoved her boot into Zagreus's side and sent him tumbling off the small cliff, though, he stepped out of the trees and quickly said, "Talisa."

Sweaty and breathing hard, Talisa turned and stared at him across the rocks. "Who are you?" A roar sounded from the valley below—one that had obviously come from the Prince of Darkness, but she didn't bother to look. Her eyes narrowed on Ryder, and she gripped the gleaming sword tighter with a hand marked in ancient Greek texts. "Where did you come from?"

Any other female would look out of place in this scene, but not her. Her long hair was pulled back in a tight tail, and a leather breastplate stamped with the seal of her forefather Herakles covered her fitted dark top and slender torso. Tight black trousers ended in knee-high black boots. There was blood and dirt and other things splattered across her skin and clothing from the battle, but she didn't seem the slightest bit afraid or disgusted. She was as confident and lethal as any warrior he'd ever met in the dream world or reality.

"My name is Morpheus."

Her violet eyes widened. "The god of dreams."

"Yes." He took a step toward her, thankful she recognized his given name. "I need your help."

"Why me?"

"Because Zakara trusts you."

Her face paled, and she lowered her sword to the ground, stepping toward him. "What's happened? Where is she?"

"Zeus took her."

"Holy *skata*."

"I don't have time to explain, but I can't get back to Olympus to rescue her without a diversion."

"Kara's my cousin. What about the Argonauts?"

He'd considered enlisting the help of the guardian warriors and rejected the idea just as quickly. "Zeus will expect them. We can't do anything to tip him off or he may hurt Zakara. If you can help me get into Olympus, I can immobilize everyone there except Zeus. Then you can get Zakara to safety while I deal with the king of the gods."

Her scrutinizing gaze skipped over his features. She was tall for a female. Only a few inches shorter than him in her boots. And, he could already tell, a finely tuned deadly weapon just waiting to strike. One he would hate to tangle with in the wrong situation. Especially since she'd just kicked the Prince of Darkness's ass.

"Tell me what you need me to do."

He breathed a quick sigh of relief. "We'll need to work fast."

* * * *

Kara shivered, unsure how long she'd been in this dark pit.

Hours had gone by. Hours in which she'd been left shivering and alone, surrounded by nothing but utter blackness. The walls of the pit were dirt, the floor uneven mounds of rock and twigs and things she didn't want to imagine that stabbed into her bare feet when she moved. She had no concept of space, didn't know how big the pit was or how far it ran beneath the surface of Olympus. The only thing she'd been able to identify when she'd been lowered into the abyss was darkness. Darkness and the smells of mildew and death that even now made her nearly gag.

She shivered again and pulled her legs closer to her body where she sat leaning against the dirt wall. There was no sense searching for a way out. Zeus would not have created an exit from the pit, not when he used it to punish his underlings. Fuzzy memories filled her mind. Memories of her cousin Elysia retelling an account of her time on Olympus with the Sirens. At one point, Elysia's mate Cerek had been thrown into a hole very similar to this while Elysia had been training with the Sirens. Except Kara distinctly remembered Elysia saying it hadn't been for a few hours or even a day. He'd been trapped in the darkness for at least a month.

Terror wrapped around her throat and squeezed tight. She shivered once more, holding onto herself tighter. She'd never survive a month in this hellhole. She'd go mad long before that time was up.

She closed her eyes, fighting back the tears. She never should have trusted Ryder. She never should have fantasized about romance and adventure. Why had she ever wanted to leave Argolea? Who cared if her life had been boring and meaningless; at least she'd been safe there. Protected. Now she had nothing. Nothing but this dank, dirty hole to remind her of how stupid she'd been. How foolish. How gullible.

The sound of metal creaking brought her eyes open. She lifted her head and squinted at the light coming toward her. Footsteps sounded, then stopped, and she held up a hand because that light was now shining directly in her eyes, blinding her.

"Get up," a male voice said. The same guard who'd brought her here hours ago. "The king of the gods wants to see you again."

Kara scrambled to her feet, thankful for any reason to get out of this pit. "Wh-where?"

He took her by the arm and turned her. "This way."

She couldn't decipher their direction, but he wove her around and through a series of tunnels until they came to a heavy steel door, which hinged open with a scream of metal scraping metal.

It was some kind of elevator. Much bigger than the cage and rope she'd been lowered into the pit from earlier. A low light above illuminated the car . As the door slammed shut behind them, she felt the lift moving upward and breathed easier knowing the darkness—for now—was behind her.

The guard handed her a damp rag. "Clean your face."

She'd prefer a shower, but the cloth felt like heaven compared to where she'd just been. As the car rumbled to a stop, she pushed the scraggly hair away from her eyes and let the male lead her into an ornate marble corridor.

The soles of her feet were sore from the pit, but she did her best to keep up as she followed. She recognized this hallway. As he turned to the right and a stone archway appeared, she realized she was right back where she'd been only hours ago, in the grotto where Zeus had questioned her before.

She swallowed hard and moved down the steps into the space. Towering trees, plants, and fountains blocked sight of the buildings surrounding the open courtyard. Above, stars twinkled in the night sky, making her think of her magical night with Ryder on that rocky lakeshore beach.

Don't think about Ryder, or Morpheus, or whatever he wants to call himself. He betrayed you. He used you and sold you off to Zeus.

Anger bubbled inside her as the guard stopped in front of a stone bench where the king of the gods was casually waiting.

"My king." The guard bowed. "Your guest."

With one hand resting on his knee, Zeus looked up and smiled. "Sit here beside me, little one. We've much to discuss."

Zakara swallowed hard as the guard disappeared into the shadows, but did as Zeus commanded, not willing to do anything to anger him right off the bat. She knew how powerful he was. She'd heard stories of his ruthlessness. Being thrown in a dark, cold pit was far from the worst thing he could do to her.

She rested her hands in her lap, hating the gauzy peach dress that was now covered in muck.

"I take it you've had plenty of time to contemplate your situation," Zeus said at her side.

"I have, my king."

"And you know what I want."

"I do."

He turned to glance down at her. "So tell me what I want to know."

"I..." Her heart raced with the only explanation she'd been able to come up with. "I did shift Ryd—I mean, Morpheus's—dreamscape into reality. Originally he'd taken me to a tropical beach, but I always preferred mountain landscapes to tropical ones, and when we were there, I pictured a place I'd fantasized about once before."

"The mountain lakeshore cabin."

"Yes."

"Had you ever been there?"

"No." She twisted her hands together in her lap. "My parents don't permit me to leave the realm of Argolea."

"For good reason, I'm sure."

For *this* very reason, but she refrained from saying so and antagonizing the god.

"So how did you know it was a real place in the Mountains of Montana in the human realm if you'd never been there?"

"I saw pictures of it in a book. We have several books about the Pacific Northwest in the castle library back in Argolea because—"

"Yes, I know." Zeus's jaw clenched. "Because the half-breeds once housed a colony there."

Technically, they were called Misos—a race of half Argolean, half human mortals—and they despised the derogatory term half-breeds. But she kept that to herself as well.

"Yes," she said instead.

Zeus pushed to his feet and stepped toward a red-flowering bush, fingering a bloom in his hand. "And what did Morpheus say when you altered his dreamscape?"

Her stomach tightened with the memory, a reaction she didn't like. "He was surprised. I didn't realize it at the time—I thought he was the one making the change—but looking back now, I realize he'd been startled that it had happened."

"I'm sure he was. Tell me"—Zeus turned—"how exactly did you

do it? Did you have to wait for Morpheus to weave the first dream, or can you alter any dream, even one of your own, into reality? Can you twist a thought or idea into reality the same way?"

"I..." Her brow lowered. Turn a thought into reality? That had dangerous implications. "I don't know. I've never done it before. It just...happened."

"I don't believe that. You're twenty-six years old. All Argoleans by your age have mastered their gifts. Tell me how it's done."

Panic swelled inside her. "I don't know. This is all new to me."

"We went around this before, little one. 'I don't know' is not an acceptable answer. Didn't your time in the pit show you that?" He dropped the bloom and moved toward her. "I want an answer. How did you alter reality?"

"I'm telling you the truth." She looked up at him, her breaths growing fast and shallow. "I don't know. If you'd just listen to me."

"I am listening to you. And what I'm hearing is defiance."

"I'm not trying to defy you."

"Refusing to answer my questions is defiance." A vein in his temple began to pulse. "No one defies me. No one says no to the king of the gods." He drew closer, looming over her like a menacing shadow, causing her to ease back on the stone bench. "Do you know what happens to those who defy me? I crush them. And make no mistake, little one. I will crush you if you don't tell me what I want to know."

She stared up at Zeus, knowing she was nothing to him. Nothing but a pawn in whatever game he wanted to play. But she was tired of being nothing. Tired of doing nothing. Out of nowhere, a strength Kara hadn't known she possessed gathered deep in her core, causing her back to straighten. "Go ahead and crush me then. Throw me back in that pit. Neither will get you the answer you want *because I don't know how I did it.* And all your ranting and raving is not going to change that fact now or anytime soon."

A low growl echoed from the king of the gods, and then he slapped his hands on the bench on both sides of her, making her gasp and lurch back.

Eyes like soulless black orbs locked on hers as he stared down at her. "You're a fool, little mortal. Are you willing to throw your life away for this?"

Was she? She swallowed hard as she stared at him. She didn't have any other answer besides, "Yes. Because it's the truth."

"Your friend Morpheus was willing to throw his life away just like this. Did he tell you about that? Did he tell you about the thousand years of misery he spent in my pit because he was unwilling to give me what I want?"

Kara's mouth fell open. "A thousand years?" she whispered.

"A thousand torturous years. Very few can last that long, but he did. I realized then the god of dreams knew how to play hardball. So I devised a way to break him."

Kara swallowed hard, almost afraid to hear more.

"If you don't care about yourself," Zeus sneered, "so be it. But you are not as strong as Morpheus, and I can be a patient god. I can wait for your loved ones to cross into the human realm. It will be satisfying torturing them in front of you until you do give in."

Kara gasped.

A victorious smile spread across Zeus's face as he leaned back. "Now you understand. I lured each and every one of Morpheus's family members out of their hiding places. I tortured and maimed his father Hypnos. His brothers Phobotor, Phantasus, and Ikelos. His mother Pasithea. I thought for sure he'd break when he heard his mother's screams, but he didn't. He is a tough one, our Morpheus. He never gave me what I wanted. And now look at him. He is the last dream weaver in the cosmos. And he works for me."

Kara's chest squeezed so tight, it was hard to get air. "Wh-what did you want from him?"

"Originally?" Zeus gazed down at his hand. "I ordered him to infiltrate Lachesis's dreams."

"The Fate?"

"The one and only."

Kara could barely believe what she was hearing. The Fates controlled all life in the cosmos. They determined births and deaths and destinies. They were more powerful than Zeus and all the gods combined.

"Morpheus refused," Zeus went on. "I'm still bitter about that. But it all worked out in my favor in the end. The dream weaver may refuse to infiltrate the dreams of immortals for me, but he does of any mortal I request. A thousand years of misery and the murder of his whole family taught him not to cross me." He dropped his hand and pinned Kara with a menacing look. "And you, little one, would be wise not to cross me as well. If you don't want your family to wind up like Morpheus's, I suggest you tell me exactly what I want to know right this very minute."

Kara's gaze dropped to the stone floor of the courtyard, but she barely saw it. All she could see was Ryder in that pit of darkness, isolated and alone for a thousand years. Being forced to watch the people he loved tortured and killed, unable to do anything to help them because he knew if he gave in to Zeus, the alternative would be a million times worse. If Zeus could infiltrate the dreams of the Fates, he could see any person's destiny—mortal or immortal. He could alter those destinies. A power like that...it would destroy the world.

Her heart felt as if it shattered into a million pieces. He'd sacrificed himself, his family, for the good of mankind. He'd done it even knowing no one would hail him as a hero or thank him down the line. How many others would do that? How many others would put the needs of many before their own wants and desires? Before the people they loved?

She didn't know anyone who could survive something like that. Who wouldn't be hardened and twisted with the need for revenge after an event so horrific. But Ryder wasn't cold and heartless. He wasn't the monster he could so easily have turned into after a history like that. He was passionate. He was gentle. When he'd come back after his walk that morning, he'd wanted nothing but to take her somewhere so she could be safe.

Safe...

The word circled in her mind. He'd wanted only to get her to safety. He must have known Zeus would come for her. He must have realized she'd been the one to shift the dreamscape into reality. And he hadn't set her up as she'd assumed. Yes, he'd been working for Zeus, but he'd told her that morning that he needed to run a quick errand before they left that cabin. He must have been talking about coming here and telling Zeus she didn't have any Horae powers. She'd heard him say that to Zeus when they'd first arrived. She'd heard the panic in his voice when Zeus had announced he didn't care and that he had other plans for her.

Warmth filled her chest. Warmth and a need to see him and tell him she knew he wasn't what Zeus said. Except...she had no idea where Zeus had sent him. And trapped here on Olympus, it was possible she might never see her fantasy again.

Unless she could fall asleep. Maybe find a way to alter her dream into reality even though she had no freakin' clue how she'd been able to do that before.

"What is that?" Zeus shot a look to the right and went still as stone. Seconds later, he growled, reached for Zakara's arm, and hauled her to her feet. "You're coming with me."

Zakara gasped and struggled against the king of the gods' hold, but he was too strong. He easily pulled her through the grotto to a different arched doorway. This one opened to the gilded main street of Olympus and the temples of the other gods.

Darkness surrounded her, illuminated only by twinkling stars and a waning moon above. But it was enough to see the bodies littering the ground. Bodies of gods and mortals completely unmoving.

She gasped, unsure what was happening. At her side, Zeus growled, "Dream weaver."

Kara looked up, and her heart nearly stopped when she spotted Ryder standing only yards away, holding a small vial of powder in his hand.

"That won't put me to sleep, you fool." Zeus shoved Kara aside and stepped down the stone steps, moving into the street across from Ryder. "You were an idiot to come back here."

"Possibly. But I'm here to offer you a deal."

Kara found her footing against the stone wall, unable to take her eyes off Ryder. He was still wearing the thin linen pants he'd had on last night, was still barefoot, his hair rumpled in the dim light. But instead of the flannel shirt he'd been wearing earlier, he was now bare chested and beautiful, the light glinting off his strong muscles and tan skin. Her perfect fantasy a thousand times over.

"And what kind of deal could you possibly offer me?" Zeus asked. "I already own you."

"You don't own me. You use me. But I choose when to say yes and when to say no. If you let Zakara return to Argolea, however, I'll give you my powers. Yours to do with as you wish."

Zeus went still. And in the silence, Kara held her breath and glanced from Ryder to Zeus and back again, confused by what this meant.

"You would give them to me freely?" Zeus asked hesitantly.

"Yes."

"With no limitations on who I could use them on?"

Oh shit. Kara's eyes flew wide. He wasn't saying—

"Yes."

No. Her chest contracted. She opened her mouth but before she could scream the word, a hand darted out of the shadows and closed over hers, yanking her to the side.

Kara grunted, but another hand slapped over her mouth, and when she twisted around in the foliage suddenly hitting her in the face, her eyes grew wide to see her cousin Talisa staring down at her.

"Shh, dammit," Talisa whispered, releasing Kara's mouth. "We're almost out of time. We have to get out of here before Zeus realizes you're gone."

They were working together. Ryder was sacrificing himself for her. He had no intention of giving his powers to Zeus. And he was willing to risk torture and another thousand years in that pit to keep her safe.

"I can't." Her throat swelled closed. "We can't leave him like this."

"It's our only chance, Kara. He's doing this for you."

She knew that. He was saving her the same way he'd saved mankind.

Only it wasn't his turn to do the saving. It was hers.

Chapter Eight

"It's a very tempting offer, dream weaver." Zeus tipped his head and leveled Ryder with a hard look. "But I think I'll pass."

Shock rippled through Ryder. "You're passing on my ability to infiltrate anyone's dreams?" That was not an answer he'd expected. "It's what you've always wanted from me."

"It was." Zeus grinned. "And I've no doubt you'll give them to me at a later date. For now I'll be content keeping you and the two Horae descendants locked up safe and sound."

Shit. He knew Talisa was trying to rescue Kara. He should have known the king of the gods wouldn't be so easily distracted.

"So go ahead and try to lock us up," Zakara said at Zeus's back, stepping out of the shadows onto the stone steps. Zeus whipped around and stared up at her. "If you can, that is."

The air seemed to move. Everything blurred, then cleared. Only when it did, they were no longer on Olympus. They were in a grassy clearing, tall trees edging the field, giant snow-capped mountains in the distance. Above stars glittered, and the sounds of night—of owls and bats, and other creatures found in the human realm—echoed on the wind.

Zeus turned a slow circle and glanced over the bodies also circling the field. All of the Argonauts, weapons already drawn and ready for a fight. Nick, the Misos leader, who was a god himself and just as powerful as Zeus. Erebus, a minor god who'd sided with the Argonauts. Prometheus, the Titan Zeus had tortured for years before he'd been freed by the Argonauts. Circe, Prometheus's mate, and the strongest witch in all the realms. And them—Talisa, Zakara, and a dream weaver.

"What is this?" Zeus growled.

"The end of you if you don't leave now," Zakara answered. "You chose not to take Ryder's deal. Now you can suffer the consequences."

Nick lifted his hands and conjured an energy bolt. Prometheus snapped his fingers and fire encircled the clearing. Circe began muttering the ancient words of a spell as the Argonauts stepped forward and circled in on the king of the gods.

Zeus's growl grew louder. His irate gaze jumped from one face to another. And then with a roar he disappeared in a plume of smoke.

"Holy Hades," Talisa whispered. "What was that?"

The Argonauts, Prometheus, Nick, Erebus, and Circe all faded until only the three of them remained.

"That," Zakara said with a smile as she turned toward her cousin, "was my gift. Pretty cool, huh?"

Talisa's wide eyes darted to her cousin's face. "You conjured that? None of them were real?"

"Well, the clearing is real. I was able to morph our reality and bring us to the human realm. But yeah, our dads and Nick and the others weren't real. I was able to tweak your perceptions and make Zeus think they were real, though."

"Holy fuck." Talisa gasped at her. "How the hell did you do that?"

"I don't know. I just focused on an image I had in my head, and it appeared. I guess it's not all that different from what I did when I was asleep. That was a dream. This was kind of like a daydream." When Talisa only stared at her, Zakara shrugged. "I don't know. It's all pretty new to me."

"That's fucking awesome. I mean...no one can do that. Do you realize how useful that's going to be?"

A satisfied smile spread across Zakara's face, but Ryder was still strung too tight to feel the same kind of elation as the girls. He grasped Zakara by the arm and pulled her into the trees. "We have to get the hell out of here before Zeus figures out what happened and comes back."

She didn't argue with him—which he was thankful for—and as soon as they were a hundred yards into the trees, he looked to Talisa and said, "Take her back to Argolea as fast as you can."

"Wait." Kara turned to face him. "You're coming with us."

"No, I'm not."

She grasped his arm when he let go of her and turned him back to face her. "Yes, you are. I didn't do all this so you could just poof out of my life again."

"Zakara..." He sighed, not wanting to argue with her, only wanting her as far from this place as possible. "Zeus will be looking for me after this. He'll be hellbent on revenge. You're not safe anywhere near me."

"I'm safe in Argolea."

"Which is why you need to go there now."

"And so are you."

"No, I'm not."

She gripped his arm tighter. "Yes, you are. Zeus can't go there."

"What do you mean?"

Her brow lowered. "Aren't you like thousands of years old? How can you not know about Zeus's one fatal design flaw?"

"I've spent my life either in the cosmos, the dream world, or in a pitch-black pit on Olympus. I didn't spend any more time than necessary focused on Zeus."

Her expression softened. "He can't access the realm of Argolea. He originally created it as a safe space for his son Herakles. A realm where his vindictive wife Hera couldn't hurt him. He banned access to Argolea from the Olympians, and in the process, he banned himself."

A place Zeus couldn't access? He stared down at her, barely believing her words. Zeus could go anywhere, even the cosmos.

She stepped into him and rested her hands on his chest. "You'll be safe in Argolea. Safer than you are in the cosmos. Zeus can find you there. He invaded your home once before. He'll do it again to get back at you."

His stomach tightened as he stared down at her in the moonlight. "You know about that?"

She nodded. "He told me. He thought it would scare me. It didn't. It just made me fall even harder for you."

His heart raced against his ribs, and his hands lifted to her arms. "I didn't hand you over to him. I wouldn't do that. I didn't even know we were in the human realm or that his Sirens could find us."

"I know that."

"I would never imprison you the way I was imprisoned. I didn't even know you could do the things you can do." He glanced past her toward the clearing he could no longer see. "That you could do...that."

"I know that too." She smiled up at him, drawing his gaze back to her beautiful face. "Which is why I want you to come home with me. Where we can both be safe. Where we can pick up where we left off in that mountain cabin."

His heart stuttered. He heard what she was saying, but could barely believe she was saying it. "I... You still want me after everything that happened?"

"Of course I do. Don't you want me?"

"Desperately, but..."

"But what?"

She looked so sweet in the moonlight. So confident and adorable at the very same time.

"But... I'm a dream weaver. I don't know anything about Argolea."

Her grin widened, and she stepped even closer, the sweet scent of her making him light headed. "So I'll teach you."

"I thought you didn't like your world. You said you weren't free there."

"I think it's safe to say my perception has changed a lot since I said that."

When he blinked down at her, her expression softened. "Freedom isn't a place, Ryder. I know that now. It's something you feel inside. And I don't hate Argolea. I love it. I love my family. I just didn't appreciate them and my place in our world. You made me see just how much I have. Just how lucky I truly am. And I want that for you. I don't want you to be alone anymore. I want you to know what it's like to be a part of something special again. Because you are special. You're extremely special, to me."

He could barely breathe from the things she was saying. The way she was saying them. The look of total adoration in her eyes when she said them.

"Um, guys?" Talisa scanned the trees. "I hate to interrupt, but we really should think about leaving."

"All you have to do is say yes," Zakara whispered, brushing her body against his in the moonlight. "Just one little yes."

He couldn't stop himself. He slid his hand into her hair and tipped her face up toward his. "I don't know. This is all happening so fast. Don't you think it's a little crazy?"

Zakara laughed, pushed to her toes, and pressed her lips against his with a kiss he felt everywhere.

"Yes, it is. Completely crazy. Which is how I know it's right." She lowered to her heels and grasped his hand, pulling her with him toward Talisa, who was already bringing her fingers together and opening a portal to Argolea, just as all the Argonauts could do.

"Are you sure about this?" he asked her as he let her pull him along, unable to look away from her. "You're going to have a lot to explain to that family of yours when you show up with a dream weaver who used to work for Zeus."

A mischievous smile curled her lips. "Someone once told me to stop worrying about what everyone else expects and to just be me. I'm finally being me, and my family's just going to have to get used to it. I'm impulsive and wild and mad for a dream weaver who turned my world upside down."

She was also talented, confident, and a force to be reckoned with. And he couldn't wait to see what she did next or where she went from here.

He stepped into her arms when she reached for him near the glow of the portal and slid his hands around her waist as he looked down at her. "Dream weavers don't know a whole lot about reality, you know."

"You'll learn." She brushed her lips against his and smiled. "Actually, I've a feeling you'll learn pretty quickly. Did I mention that my father is an Argonaut? A big one? And that I'm his only daughter?"

His steps slowed, and he playfully pulled back on her waist. "On second thought..."

She grinned and tugged him toward the portal. "Oh, and he's immortal, just like you. He's descended from Achilles's line. You're gonna love him. He, however, will probably take a while to warm up to you."

Ryder frowned, but didn't stop her from drawing him forward. "Something tells me I would have been safer staying with Zeus. Are you sure you don't want to weave a new reality for us?"

She laughed. "Baby, *you* are my new reality. And I can't wait to get you home so we can both start living it."

Home.

That was a dream he'd all but given up on. As the portal popped and light flashed around them, he leaned down and kissed her, so very thankful she'd lured him out of the cosmos and into her fantasies.

Reality was a thousand times better than any dream he could ever weave.

And because of her, the dream he thought would never be real had finally come true.

Epilogue

A whisper-soft touch grazed the back of Zakara's neck, making her smile where she lay softly dozing against her pillow. Warm early morning rays of sunlight slid over her and the big four-poster bed in her bedroom suite in the castle in Argolea. A very warm, very hard male body pressed up against her spine, and those tempting lips of his found a new spot to tickle and kiss on the side of her throat.

"Mm..." She reached down and wrapped her hand around Ryder's fingers, which were already sliding under the hem of the tank at her waist. "If either of my parents find you in here, they're going to skin you alive."

"Your mother likes me, *fantasía*. And your father's still out with the Argonauts on assignment. And for the record, you're the one who lured me into this bed with you by shifting your dream into reality. I was innocently minding my own business in my room down the hall before you started all that weaving."

"Ha!" She quickly rolled and pushed him to his back so she could climb over him. Wrapping her hands around his wrists, she pinned his arms to the mattress and smiled down. "You're the one who did the weaving and the luring. Though I did like that new thing you did in my dream with your tongue."

He chuckled, lifted his head, and captured her lips for a quick kiss. "I could tell. I'm pretty sure you're going to enjoy it way more here in our reality."

She sighed and opened, letting go of his wrists so she could slide down and kiss him deeper. So she could feel him against her everywhere. She knew she was going to enjoy it more here. Though she loved when he found her in her dreams, something he enjoyed teasing her with when they were apart, the reality of his body against hers, of his lips consuming hers, of his heat and strength and familiar scent overwhelming her was a million times better than any fantasy. It was for him too.

"Ah, *fantasía,*" he whispered against her mouth. His hands landed on her hips, then slid down to cup her ass and pull her against his growing erection. "If you keep that up, your father is most definitely going to find me here in this bed with you. And then I'll be forced to tell him what a vixen his daughter is."

She laughed and drew back a breath from his lips. "You wouldn't dare."

His heated gaze skipped over her features, then he grinned. A full blown mesmerizing smile that was so relaxed and happy, it made him ten thousand times more attractive then he already was. "No, I wouldn't. I don't want to give him any reason to cancel our binding ceremony tomorrow. After three long, agonizing months, I finally got you to say yes to being mine. I'm not about to let anyone get in the way of that."

She chuckled and kissed him again. "You are a persistent god, I will give you that." She eased back once more, her smile fading. "Are you sure about this? We don't have to be bound. You've barely had time to get settled in Argolea, and—"

"Yes, I'm sure." He lifted his head and pressed a kiss against her bare shoulder. "I want you. I've wanted you since the first moment you lured me into your dreams. And now that we've gotten to know each other better, I'm more than sure I want you forever." He met her gaze with spellbinding eyes swirling like the cosmos. "I love you, *fantasía.* I want to spend my life with you. And I want that life to start now."

Her heart felt as if it filled to bursting. Never in her life had she expected this—him. Yes, she'd dreamt about that elusive happily ever after, but she'd never thought it could be real. Not for her.

"I love you too," she whispered. Sliding back down so they were pressed together, chest to chest, she skimmed her fingertips over the soft stubble on his jaw and pressed her lips against his once more. "I love you endlessly. I just wanted to be sure you weren't having any second thoughts."

He opened at the first touch and drew her into a toe-curling kiss she felt everywhere. "No second thoughts," he mumbled against her mouth. "Not about the binding ceremony. Though that is an odd word for what's basically a wedding. And it gives me all kinds of ideas about the next dreamscape I'm going to weave for you. One where you're wearing a sexy white negligee and veil, with your hands bound in front of you, and your luscious body bent over a spanking bench."

She jerked back and pressed her fingers against his ribs, making him squirm beneath her. "Oh, you'd better not, dream weaver."

He laughed as she tickled him, but she wasn't quick enough to climb off him. He wrapped an arm around her waist and flipped her to her back before she could get away.

Sinking his teeth into her throat, he gently bit down, then sucked the spot until she moaned. "Mm, I love twisting your fantasies."

She knew he did. He loved pushing her—sexually and emotionally. And she loved him for it. Loved everything he did for and to her. Her hands landed against his sides, and she sighed as he kissed his way up her neck.

He drew back and gazed down at her. "But I love being here in the real world with you more. And I can't wait to be your *pantreménos.*"

Husband.

Her whole body warmed at the word, and any worry she had about her parents finding him in her room this early faded from her mind. She lifted her head and skimmed her lips against his, aching to feel him everywhere. "I can't wait for that either. I don't want to wait. Show me what kind of *pantreménos* you're going to be. Show me right now."

He groaned and sank into her, kissing her deeply and with every bit of passion she felt in her own soul for him. She licked into his mouth, savoring the taste of him against her tongue, and slid her hands down his muscular spine to the waistband at his hips. But before she could even push the sweats down so she could feel him right where she ached for him most, a knock sounded at the door, followed by her mother's familiar voice calling, "Zakara? Are you awake?"

Ryder stilled and quietly drew back from her lips, staring down at her in the early morning light. "Busted," he whispered. "You were right. Quick, alter this reality before your father shows up and kills me."

She couldn't stop herself from grinning. "You're on your own with that one, *ómorfos.*" She kissed him quickly, then dropped her head back down to the pillow and called, "Yes, I'm awake. I'll be right out."

He frowned and moved off her, and as she pushed to her feet and shook out the legs of her pajama bottoms, she said, "Try not to look so delightfully rumpled. That won't help matters." Fluffing her hair out, she shot a look at the bulge behind his sweats. "And don't come out until that thing's long gone. If my father sees *that*, he will skin you, impending binding or not. None of my perception altering abilities will be able to help you in that situation."

"Ha ha, very funny." He tipped his head and waved his hand. "Go already so I can. You make me freakin' hard every time you tease me."

She was still grinning when she tugged the door open and slipped into the living room, pulling it closed behind her. Thankfully, her father was nowhere to be seen. Only her mother stood near the stone fireplace, studying a picture Kara had recently framed of her and Ryder.

"I like this." Callia skimmed her finger over the white frame surrounding the picture of the two of them smiling in the sunshine, water shimmering at their backs, jagged snow-capped mountains in the distance. "When did you take it?"

"Last week. Up at the lake."

The "lake" was the Tyrrhenian Sea, in the northern reaches of Argolea. Where she'd taken Ryder to show him her parents' cabin—a cabin that was eerily similar to the one where they'd spent an amazing night together. It was also where he'd asked her to bind his life to hers.

"I thought so." Her mother smiled. "Did he like it up there?"

Now that her parents knew she could alter perceptions, they weren't so concerned about her out and about in the wilds on her own. Even if some of Zeus's Sirens found a way to sneak into their realm, Zeus himself couldn't get here, and they and her parents knew she could take care of herself—heck, she'd proven that to everyone. But they still worried. Which, she figured, was exactly what parents were supposed to do. And instead of making her feel confined now, that knowledge made her heart swell.

"He loved it. We're planning to go back for a few days after the binding ceremony."

"I think that's a great idea. You two deserve some peace and quiet after everything you've been through." Her mother stepped toward her. "Before everything gets crazy with all the pre-binding festivities, I just wanted you to know how happy I am for you. And proud. You might not have my healing gift, but your gift is just as important. And I'm thrilled you and Ryder are using your gifts for the good of others. I knew one day you'd find what you were meant to do with your life."

Pride swept through Kara. Her mother wasn't talking about her being Ryder's wife. She was talking about the new clinic she and Ryder were opening after they got back from their vacation. It had actually been her idea, and she had no idea if it was going to work, but she knew there were others in their realm struggling with hopes and dreams and just what their purpose was in this world. No, she wasn't a healer, but she understood depression and anxiety, what it felt like not to fit in, and just what altering perceptions could do for a person's self-esteem. And Ryder was an expert on dreams and their interpretations. He was the one who was really going to help their patients. She still had a lot to learn about mental health, but for the first time in her life, she was excited about that learning. And she was looking forward to finally having a purpose.

"Thanks. That means a lot to me."

Her mother wrapped her arms around Kara's shoulders and hugged her. "I'm always proud of you, Kara. No matter what."

Kara closed her eyes and hugged her mother back, so very thankful for her family. They weren't a burden as she'd once thought. They were a blessing. A blessing she would never take for granted again.

"Now." Gripping her shoulders, her mother eased back and looked down at her. "We have a lot to do to get ready for tomorrow. Which means Ryder needs to get himself out of your room so we can do them."

Kara chuckled, not the least bit worried that her mother knew he was in there. "Got it."

"And your father's waiting outside in the hall for you."

"He's back from his mission?" Kara's eyes widened. He'd been out with the Argonauts for the last seven days. She knew her mother had informed him about the binding, but she hadn't had a chance to tell him herself. "Why didn't he come in?"

Her mother dropped her hands and rolled her eyes. "Because he's old fashioned. He'd rather go on thinking you're his baby girl, not a grown woman."

Meaning he didn't want to find her in bed with Ryder. "I'll always be his baby girl."

"I know." Her mother's face softened. "Go tell him that. I'll kick your man out so we can get started. The sooner he learns the women rule this family, the better."

Kara's lips curled in a smile as she moved toward the main door. "I agree. He has no idea what he's about to get into."

Callia grinned. "No, he doesn't. Lucky man."

Kara was still smiling when she stepped into the wide marble corridor of the castle and spotted her father pacing near several Grecian columns, his broad shoulders filling out the dark shirt he wore, his blond hair, just like hers, catching the light, making him look more angelic than warrior.

His feet stilled the second he heard her, and he turned to look her way. And the second his silvery eyes met hers, it was as if no time had passed. She was five years old again, running across the lawn toward him as he walked up their drive after a full day running missions with the Argonauts. She used to watch for him from the windows of their house outside Tiyrns every day. Couldn't wait 'til he got home. Couldn't imagine life without him. He'd been her first love. The only man at the center of her world for a very long time. And she suddenly wanted him to know he would always have a place there. Her binding with Ryder would never change that.

"*Pampas.*" She threw herself into his arms and hugged him tightly as he held her. "I'm so glad you're back."

"I'm glad too." His arms felt like steel bands around her. "I missed you."

She'd missed him too. She always did when he was gone. This time more than ever. Her eyes grew misty. "You're not upset, are you? About the binding? About it happening so fast? We wanted to tell you sooner, but..."

"Of course not." He drew back and looked down at her. "All I ever wanted was for you to be happy. And if he makes you happy, then I'm glad, baby girl."

"He does. Very much."

"Good." He brushed a tear from her cheek she hadn't known had slipped free. "And I already knew. Ryder asked me for my blessing before I left."

"He did?"

Zander nodded. "He's not so bad, your dream weaver. I'm getting used to him. Slowly."

Kara chuckled and glanced down at his thick, dark shirt, knowing he was teasing. But there was a thread of truth in his words. It was hard for him to let go. And part of her didn't want him to. "I think he's still a little scared of you."

"As well he should be. I am an Argonaut who can't be killed."

She smirked.

"And if he ever gets out of line I've got a long list of Argonauts on my side who'll show him the proper way."

She couldn't help herself, she laughed. "Trust me, if he ever steps out of line, I'll be the first one to show him the proper way."

Zander's lips curled. "I know you will. Just as I know you can take care of yourself. You are my daughter, after all."

She gazed up at him, completely bewildered that she'd ever thought her parents were disappointed in her. "I'll always be your daughter, *pampas*. Nothing and no one can ever change that. Not time, not the future, not even my love for Ryder."

"I know you will, *chará*." He smiled. "And you will always have a place with us, no matter where life takes you. This is your home, Zakara."

She pressed her cheek against his chest and closed her eyes as she hugged him close. He was right. This was her home. *He* was her home. And her home was finally complete now that she'd found Ryder.

She no longer yearned to escape into her dreams. Everything she would ever need was right here, waiting for her in the real world.

* * * *

Also from 1001 Dark Nights and Elisabeth Naughton Hunted, Ravaged, Unchained, and Surrender.

Eternal Guardians Lexicon

Argolea. Realm established by Zeus for the blessed heroes and their descendants

Argonauts. Eternal guardian warriors who protect Argolea. In every generation, one from the original seven bloodlines (Heracles, Achilles, Jason, Odysseus, Perseus, Theseus, and Bellerophon) is chosen to continue the guardian tradition.

binding. Marriage

chará. Term of endearment; my joy

Cosmic Deities. Minor gods who dwell in the cosmos.

Fates. Three goddesses who control the thread of life for all mortals from birth until death

Horae. Three goddesses of balance controlling life and order

matéras. Mother

Misos. Half-human/half-Argolean race that lives hidden among humans.

Olympians. Current ruling gods of the Greek pantheon, led by Zeus; meddle in human life.

omorfos. Handsome

Oneiroi. Realm of dreams in the center of the cosmos

oraios. Beautiful

pampas. Daddy

pantreménos. Husband.

Siren Order. Zeus's elite band of personal warriors. Commanded by Athena

skata. Swearword

Titans. The ruling gods before the Olympians

Sign up for the 1001 Dark Nights Newsletter
and be entered to win a Tiffany Key necklace.

There's a contest every month!

Go to www.1001DarkNights.com to subscribe.

As a bonus, all subscribers can download
FIVE FREE exclusive books!

Discover 1001 Dark Nights Collection Six

Go to www.1001DarkNights.com for more information.

DRAGON CLAIMED by Donna Grant
A Dark Kings Novella

ASHES TO INK by Carrie Ann Ryan
A Montgomery Ink: Colorado Springs Novella

ENSNARED by Elisabeth Naughton
An Eternal Guardians Novella

EVERMORE by Corinne Michaels
A Salvation Series Novella

VENGEANCE by Rebecca Zanetti
A Dark Protectors/Rebels Novella

ELI'S TRIUMPH by Joanna Wylde
A Reapers MC Novella

CIPHER by Larissa Ione
A Demonica Underworld Novella

RESCUING MACIE by Susan Stoker
A Delta Force Heroes Novella

ENCHANTED by Lexi Blake
A Masters and Mercenaries Novella

TAKE THE BRIDE by Carly Phillips
A Knight Brothers Novella

INDULGE ME by J. Kenner
A Stark Ever After Novella

THE KING by Jennifer L. Armentrout
A Wicked Novella

QUIET MAN by Kristen Ashley
A Dream Man Novella

ABANDON by Rachel Van Dyken
A Seaside Pictures Novella

THE OPEN DOOR by Laurelin Paige
A Found Duet Novella

CLOSER by Kylie Scott
A Stage Dive Novella

SOMETHING JUST LIKE THIS by Jennifer Probst
A Stay Novella

BLOOD NIGHT by Heather Graham
A Krewe of Hunters Novella

TWIST OF FATE by Jill Shalvis
A Heartbreaker Bay Novella

MORE THAN PLEASURE YOU by Shayla Black
A More Than Words Novella

WONDER WITH ME by Kristen Proby
A With Me In Seattle Novella

THE DARKEST ASSASSIN by Gena Showalter
A Lords of the Underworld Novella

Also from 1001 Dark Nights:
DAMIEN by J. Kenner

Discover 1001 Dark Nights

Go to www.1001DarkNights.com for more information.

COLLECTION THREE
HIDDEN INK by Carrie Ann Ryan
BLOOD ON THE BAYOU by Heather Graham
SEARCHING FOR MINE by Jennifer Probst
DANCE OF DESIRE by Christopher Rice
ROUGH RHYTHM by Tessa Bailey
DEVOTED by Lexi Blake
Z by Larissa Ione
FALLING UNDER YOU by Laurelin Paige
EASY FOR KEEPS by Kristen Proby
UNCHAINED by Elisabeth Naughton
HARD TO SERVE by Laura Kaye
DRAGON FEVER by Donna Grant
KAYDEN/SIMON by Alexandra Ivy/Laura Wright
STRUNG UP by Lorelei James
MIDNIGHT UNTAMED by Lara Adrian
TRICKED by Rebecca Zanetti
DIRTY WICKED by Shayla Black
THE ONLY ONE by Lauren Blakely
SWEET SURRENDER by Liliana Hart

COLLECTION FOUR
ROCK CHICK REAWAKENING by Kristen Ashley
ADORING INK by Carrie Ann Ryan
SWEET RIVALRY by K. Bromberg
SHADE'S LADY by Joanna Wylde
RAZR by Larissa Ione
ARRANGED by Lexi Blake
TANGLED by Rebecca Zanetti
HOLD ME by J. Kenner
SOMEHOW, SOME WAY by Jennifer Probst
TOO CLOSE TO CALL by Tessa Bailey
HUNTED by Elisabeth Naughton
EYES ON YOU by Laura Kaye
BLADE by Alexandra Ivy/Laura Wright
DRAGON BURN by Donna Grant
TRIPPED OUT by Lorelei James

About Elisabeth Naughton

Before topping multiple bestseller lists—including those of the New York Times, USA Today, and the Wall Street Journal—Elisabeth Naughton taught middle school science. A voracious reader, she soon discovered she had a knack for creating stories with a chemistry of their own. The spark turned into a flame, and Naughton now writes full-time. Elisabeth has penned over thirty novels and writes in multiple genres, including paranormal romance, romantic suspense, and contemporary romance. Her books have been translated into numerous languages and have earned several award nominations, including three prestigious RITA® nominations from Romance Writers of America. In 2017, REPRESSED, the first book in her Deadly Secrets series, won the RITA® for best romantic suspense. When not dreaming up new stories, Naughton can be found spending time with her husband and three children in their western Oregon home. Learn more at www.ElisabethNaughton.com.

Discover More Elisabeth Naughton

Hunted: An Eternal Guardians Novella
By Elisabeth Naughton

Erebus–*Dark in every sense of the word, a skilled and lethal warrior, and sinfully sexy by design.*

Since the dawn of modern man, Erebus was Hades' secret weapon in the war between the immortal realms. Until Hades lost the minor god in a bet to his older brother Zeus. For the last hundred years, Erebus has trained Zeus's Siren warriors in warfare and the sexual arts. But he's never stopped longing for freedom. For a life filled with choice. And lately, he also longs for one Siren who entranced him during their steamy seduction sessions. A nymph he quickly became obsessed with and who was ripped from his grasp when her seduction training was complete. One he's just learned Zeus has marked for death because she failed the last Siren test.

Before Erebus can intercede on the nymph's behalf, she escapes Olympus and flees into the human realm. In a fit of rage, Zeus commands Erebus to hunt her down and kill her. Erebus sees his opportunity to finally go after what *he* wants, but he's torn. Freedom means nothing if the Siren at the center of his fantasies doesn't truly crave him back. Because defying the gods will unleash the fury of Olympus, and if he chooses her over his duty, whether she joins him in exile or not, the hunter will become the hunted.

* * * *

Ravaged: An Eternal Guardians Novella
By Elisabeth Naughton

Ari — Once an Eternal Guardian, now he's nothing but a rogue mercenary with one singular focus: revenge. His guardian brothers all think he's dead, but he is very much alive in the human realm, chipping away at Zeus's Sirens every chance he can, reveling in his brutality and anonymity. Until, that is, he abducts the wrong female and his identity is finally exposed. It will take more than the Eternal Guardians, more even than the gods to rein Ari in after everything he's done. It may just take the courage of one woman willing to stand up to a warrior who's become a savage.

* * * *

Unchained: An Eternal Guardians Novella
By Elisabeth Naughton

PROMETHEUS – One of the keenest Titans to ever walk the earth. Until, that is, his weakness for the human race resulted in his imprisonment.

For thousands of years, Prometheus's only certainty was his daily torture at Zeus's hand. Now, unchained by the Eternal Guardians, he spends his days in solitude, trying to forget the past. He's vowed no allegiance in the war between mortal and immortal, but when a beautiful maiden seeks him out and begs for his help, he's once again powerless to say no. Soon, Prometheus is drawn into the very conflict he swore to avoid, and, to save the maiden's life, he must choose sides. But she has a secret of her own, and if Prometheus doesn't discover what she's hiding in time, the world won't simply find itself embroiled in a battle between good and evil, it will fall in total domination to Prometheus's greatest enemy.

* * * *

Surrender: A House of Sin Novella
By Elisabeth Naughton

The leaders of my House want her dead.

The men I've secretly aligned myself with want her punished for screwing up their coup.

I've been sent by both to deal with her, but one look at the feisty redhead and I've got plans of my own.

Before I carry out anyone else's orders, she's going to give me what I want. And only when I'm satisfied will I decide if she lives or dies.

Depending, of course, on just how easily she surrenders...

Hunted

An Eternal Guardians Novella
By Elisabeth Naughton
Now Available

Erebus—*Dark in every sense of the word, a skilled and lethal warrior, and sinfully sexy by design.*

Since the dawn of modern man, Erebus was Hades' secret weapon in the war between the immortal realms. Until Hades lost the minor god in a bet to his older brother Zeus. For the last hundred years, Erebus has trained Zeus's Siren warriors in warfare and the sexual arts. But he's never stopped longing for freedom. For a life filled with choice. And lately, he also longs for one Siren who entranced him during their steamy seduction sessions. A nymph he quickly became obsessed with and who was ripped from his grasp when her seduction training was complete. One he's just learned Zeus has marked for death because she failed the last Siren test.

Before Erebus can intercede on the nymph's behalf, she escapes Olympus and flees into the human realm. In a fit of rage, Zeus commands Erebus to hunt her down and kill her. Erebus sees his opportunity to finally go after what *he* wants, but he's torn. Freedom means nothing if the Siren at the center of his fantasies doesn't truly crave him back. Because defying the gods will unleash the fury of Olympus, and if he chooses her over his duty, whether she joins him in exile or not, the hunter will become the hunted.

* * * *

"Since you're out of bed," Erebus said, drawing closer, "you must be feeling better."

"Better?" Sera inched backward until her spine hit the wall. "I-I wouldn't say better, per say. Just...worried."

Worried? About him? He wished she was, but considering she looked like a cornered animal at the moment, he didn't believe her for a second. "Well, for what I have planned I don't really need you better, just able to stand upright."

Her eyes widened. "What you have planned?"

Was that excitement he heard in her voice? Oh, he definitely liked that.

He braced a hand against the wall over her shoulder and leaned into all her seductive heat. "Why do you think I nursed you back to health? So we could finish what we started the other day."

She sucked in a breath and held completely still. "You don't mean—"

"I mean exactly that, female." He hefted her over his shoulder, ignoring her wiggle and the yelp that passed over her lips, and headed straight for the main staircase. "We have unfinished business, and now that you're well enough, we're going to get back to it."

Her hands landed against his back. Warm and small and so damn enticing. She tried to push herself upright, but he held on tight to her legs, keeping her immobile as he carried her up the stairs.

"B—but," she sputtered. "I have a concussion!"

"Then I guess you should have stayed in bed."

A warm glow emanated from the fireplace in her room as he drew close, bathing the corridor in an eerie orange light. He moved into the room and dropped her to her feet in front of the same corner bedpost he'd tied her to originally, then he reached for the charmed rope that was still wrapped around the wood. "Hold still."

"Erebus, you can't do this!"

She struggled, but his forearm at her chest kept her immobile as he bound her to the post. When he was done, he stepped back, perched his hands on his hips, and eyed her carefully. "This looks very familiar. Though this time I'm going to do more than just leave you alone to plot your escape."

Her eyes shot daggers into his as he grabbed a chair, dragged it in front of her, turned it around and straddled the seat. Resting his forearms on the back, he watched as she struggled to break free. Smirked at the way her long, silky blonde hair fall over her eyes and the delicate skin of her face. And smiled as she grew more outraged by the second.

"We can do this the easy way or we can do this the hard way, Sera, but know this, you're not getting away from me until I'm ready to let you go. And I have no intention of letting you go until you give me what I want."

She glared hard in his direction. "I'm not giving you anything. If you want it, you're going to have to try to take it from me."

Excitement pulsed inside him. That was exactly the answer he'd hoped for. After twiddling his thumbs for the last two days, waiting for her heal and regain her strength, he was more than ready for some fun. And if memory served, fun with Sera was hotter than anything he'd had before or since her.

Grinning, he pushed up off the chair. "I guess we're doing this the hard way then. Good thing that was my first choice."

On behalf of 1001 Dark Nights,

Liz Berry and M.J. Rose would like to thank ~

Steve Berry
Doug Scofield
Kim Guidroz
Jillian Stein
InkSlinger PR
Dan Slater
Asha Hossain
Chris Graham
Fedora Chen
Kasi Alexander
Jessica Johns
Dylan Stockton
Richard Blake
and Simon Lipskar

9832

50500921R00064

Made in the USA
Columbia, SC
07 February 2019